P9-DMR-398

my russian love

Also by Dan Franck

Separation

Nan A. Talese

Doubleday

New York London Toronto

Sydney Auckland

my
russian
love

Dan Franck

Translated from the French
by Jon Rothschild

PUBLISHED BY NAN A. TALESE
an imprint of Doubleday
a division of Bantam Doubleday Dell Publishing Group, Inc.
1540 Broadway, New York, New York 10036

DOUBLEDAY is a trademark of Doubleday, a division of
Bantam Doubleday Dell Publishing Group, Inc.

Book design by Maria Carella

Library of Congress Cataloging-in-Publication Data
Franck, Dan.
    [Jeune fille. English]
  My Russian love / Dan Franck; translated from the French
by Jon Rothschild.
      p.   cm.
  I. Rothschild, Jon.   II. Title.
PQ2666.R2664J4813   1997
843'.914—dc20   96-20630
                                                        CIP

ISBN 0-385-48488-7

Printed in the United States of America

February 1997

First Edition

10   9   8   7   6   5   4   3   2   1

For Marion

For Fabienne and Enki

No, I wasn't under foreign skies,
Nor shielded by foreign wings.
I was with my people,
Where my people were, in their misery.

—*Anna Akhmatova*

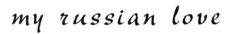

my russian love

The train had just passed through a town whose name he didn't know when he saw her hand. He'd been staring up at the patterns on the face of the pale, round moon that hung over the darkened landscape, trying to locate the Sea of Humors and the Ocean of Storms.

It wasn't so much her hand he saw as the movement of her arm reflected in the glass. She was sitting across the aisle five rows ahead of him, legs crossed under the table, wearing a black dress and a big silk shawl, also black. Her long, straight hair, dark brown and magnificent, spilled over the shawl. He glimpsed her profile—the shadow of a cheek, the arc of her nose—but never saw her mouth, much less her smile or the glitter of her eyes.

Five rows seemed a long way, but he saw the gesture clearly, first outlined in the window and then, as he turned to look, her wrist, her arm, her fingers. She brought one hand to the nape of her neck, tilted her head back, and drew her opposite shoulder forward to her cheek, as though gripping her face in a painful embrace.

All at once he felt scents waft over him, bearing a yearning he thought was gone, one he'd long tried to evade. He never expected it might happen like this, or even that it might happen at all. He had shrouded her memory in a veil impervious to feeling. She was a presence nestled within him, a localized pain he never prodded.

But now the stone wedged between her memory and the rocking of the train suddenly crumbled.

She stood up, slung her purse strap over her shoulder, quickly smoothed her hair with her fingers, and disappeared down the aisle without so much as a glance at the few remaining passengers.

He stood up too. He felt a chill when he realized that the two of them had crossed half of Europe together on this train that had set out from St. Petersburg and would arrive in Paris at dawn.

one

He saw her for the first time in a café in a Paris suburb one Monday in November. He'd come to play chess. In those days he was studying for the entrance exam to film school, supporting himself by playing chess for fifty francs a game. He never lost.

He'd gone into the back room of the café, where an opponent waited for him.

The room had a coal-burning stove, a jukebox, and a few rectangular tables, one of which had been reserved for him. At other tables near the windows old men leaned over chessboards supplied by the management. There were timers alongside the boards, and the rhythmic slapping of the buttons made a background noise of dull thuds and barely perceptible clicks.

When he came in, she was seated at a table in the back, near the jukebox, listening to Bob Dylan's "Mr. Tambourine Man." He noticed her immediately. She wore a kilt and a black turtleneck sweater. She was smoking a cigarette and drinking an espresso, without sugar; he could tell by the way she grimaced slightly with each sip. She was with two boys and another girl as young as she was. They all turned to look at him except her. A stack of books and notebooks bound by two crossed rubber straps lay on the table in front of her.

She had long brown hair and a matte complexion. Her sweater seemed to be mohair, perhaps cashmere—a fabric so warm it made you want to touch it. It was cold outside, and he would now always think of autumn as a cozy season of soft, thick turtlenecks revealing the tiniest patch of skin, a dream of promised intimacy.

She was the last to look up—not because of him, but because the needle of the jukebox got stuck. She told him later that the first thing she noticed about him was that, like her, he was dressed in black, and that his wrinkled raincoat made him seem unusually tall.

He stood motionless, staring into a vivid blue gaze that gripped him with a kind of violence. It was impossible to look away.

He forgot—or no longer cared—why he had come. All he wanted was to walk over to the girl, take her by the hand, and lead her away.

She blinked first, crushing her cigarette out in a yellow ashtray and turning back to her friends. People started talking again. He sat down opposite his opponent, a man in his sixties whose silver hair blended perfectly with his cream-colored breast-pocket handkerchief, his pearl-gray suit, his quietly pretentious manners. He had a stiff, aristocratic bearing that exuded the condescending benevolence of a bourgeois of plebeian descent. A Yankee smile and a cold eye.

They played a very long game whose subtleties he was later unable to recall. All he knew was that he had lost, tipping over his king in unprecedented capitulation. When he looked up, she was gone. He went over to her table. All that was left of her were a few cigarette butts, one of them still smoldering. She smoked Gitane filters.

At nine the next morning he went back to the café. He played "Mr. Tambourine Man" on the jukebox and sat down at the table she'd taken the day before.

He ordered a tea. When the song was over, he left the café for another venue, where another opponent awaited him. This time he won in less than fifteen moves. He made arrangements for a game the next day and spent the afternoon wandering around.

At five that evening he walked into the café, sat at the same table, and waited.

It was just getting dark when she came in, alone, wearing a dark overcoat, her hair hidden under a suede hat trimmed with fur. She carried her books under her arm. The cold had flecked her cheeks with little red spots that brightened her face.

She saw him but didn't acknowledge him. She went to a table near the stove, slipped off her coat, and sat down. She rubbed her hands to warm them, took off her hat, shook her head to free her hair. And when it spilled down over her shoulders, she made that gesture: fingers gripping the nape of her neck, head tilted back, elbow bent, upper arm drawn up against her cheek to form a kind of frame that cradled her head. She closed her eyes. It was a gesture of deep weariness bordering on distress, a silent lament that moved him.

When she straightened up, he stood. She ordered a warm milk, peeled the rubber straps off her books, opened a notebook, and began to draw. He went to the jukebox and put on "Mr. Tambourine Man." He sat back down, took out a portable chess set, and was soon engrossed in replaying a game pitting Alekhine against Nimzovich at the 1925 tournament in Bled, Yugoslavia.

On the third day she didn't show up. By six o'clock he realized she wasn't coming, but he stayed anyway, not waiting for her, but trying to conjure her silhouette in cigarette smoke. He tilted his head back, put his hand on the nape of his neck, and closed his eyes. That's what she does, he thought to himself.

He played "Mr. Tambourine Man" over and over again until another customer begged him to pick another tune. Then he paid the check and left. It was dark out. Fog crept along the sidewalks and seeped under people's coats, swelling up inside them and gnawing like the blues.

He went to the station, bought a ticket, and caught the first train for Paris.

When he felt a veil of sadness numbing him, he headed for Saint-Michel in search of light and noise. He went into a club, sat at a table by himself, and let the music rock him as he sat hunched over his drink, face slack, eyes closed—like the girl in black. And, like her, he waited for the weight of his troubles to fall at his feet. His mind was enveloped in a mist that felt like steam, or water, or clouds, a silky curtain of unearned sorrow, a lifeless backdrop against which logic was helpless. It could be blotted out only by colors of another hue. Ambient noise versus private silence.

At dawn he took the train back to the suburbs, standing erect amid his own decay, battling the urge to bury himself that overtook him when he looked right and left at the swaying silhouettes of people just like him. He let himself be lulled by the clacking of the wheels. He stared out at the landscape, looking at the very things he looked at now, in this empty, over-heated compartment: an overcast sky, darkened houses, and the slow, barely ordered movements of a still slumbering story.

On the sixth day he sat at a table off to the side. He had just won his first game of the day when the girl came in. She stopped in the doorway and looked around. She seemed tense, but when she saw him her face relaxed. He thought he detected the hint of a smile. She was empty-handed. No books today. She didn't look for a place to sit down. She just waited for him.

He got up and went to her, gazing into those

very blue eyes and glancing at the tip of her white scarf. She wore a touch of perfume.

"I was sick yesterday," she said.

He recognized the accent immediately.

They left. He wished it was the dead of night, so they could walk down cold, deserted streets, barely visible in a blanket of fog. But that's not the way it was. The gray streets were lined with parked cars. The buildings were dirty. Dogs barked. The bare branches of a few trees hung over the bus stop.

He tucked the chessboard under his arm and put his hands in his coat pockets to stop himself from doing anything rash—taking her hand, making her stop, turning her to him, pulling her tight against his chest, his hands in her hair.

"You're Russian," he blurted awkwardly. "From Moscow, right?" When she didn't reply, he tried other cities—Kiev, Riga, Alma-Ata.

She stared at him, astonished. "People never recognize my accent," she said.

"My grandfather was from the Black Sea."

They made their way up a twisting slope with sidewalks too narrow for them to walk side by side. He stepped into the road. Now and then a passing car forced him closer to her, but he moved back into the street as soon as possible. He listened not so much to her words as to her tone, and to the boundless charm he glimpsed behind the words.

"I was born in Leningrad," she said. "My parents are still there. My mother's French. I've been living with her sister for a year now."

She said she was in her freshman year, that she was studying literature, and that she wanted to teach, maybe in Russia, maybe not. She'd never been to France before. Her dream was to see the Mediterranean. She spoke in an intonation he would always remember with emotion, her voice now serious, now singsong, sometimes sliding toward shrillness. Then the reticence vanished and she became animated, moving her head and hands, laughing.

He asked why she'd left Russia, and she said, "To get out." There was a sadness, a gravity, in her voice, and for the moment he let it drop. He wanted her to tell him her real secrets the next time they met—if she was drawn to him as he was to her. They trudged up a steep path to one of those fashionable residences for mid-level managers who couldn't afford Paris but wanted something nearby and comfortable. Anyway, they liked to claim, ten years from now Paris will be out here, or near enough.

They got to know each other quickly, in scattered bits and pieces. She wanted to know if he played chess all the time and seemed surprised when he said he didn't. "But you play even when you're alone! You must be crazy to sit in front of a board like that when no one else is there."

He laughed. He told her he was going to take a test to get into film school.

"Why film school?"

"Because I want to make movies."

"So what's the chess for?"

"A temporary profession."

"I'm glad it's only temporary."

He asked why. She stopped, turned to him, and exclaimed, "Because it's not a profession, that's why!"

Her cheeks were flushed and her fists were on her hips. He hoped he would see her again tomorrow and the next day and every day after that. He wanted to touch her face, take her hand. But he didn't. He wondered if she was a virgin, if she would kiss him when they parted, or shake his hand, or just say, "See you." Would she give him her phone number? Would she meet him at the café again?

They went through a gate beyond which stretched a string of small, low buildings.

"That's where I live," the girl said, pointing to a cream-colored structure.

She stopped at the top of a staircase and said, "My room's on the fifth floor. Third window from the right."

"I see it," he said.

"Bye."

He put his hand out. She shrugged and pecked him on the cheek.

"Tomorrow we'll tell each other different things."

She stared at him with a touch of mockery in her eyes. Or maybe it was interest, he wasn't sure. Then she whirled, hurried to a green door, and disappeared.

He stood there wondering whether he'd said enough or too much, whether he'd feel more at ease next time, whether it had been a good idea to walk her home. And whether the exhilaration he felt was like love, happiness, poetry—or death.

He went home. He lived in a garden-level apartment rented from a widow who lived on the two upper
floors of a house whose damp smell he still recalled
twenty years later whenever he went into an uninhab-
ited country house. It was a smell that seemed to
plunge him into the acrid, bitter waters of late adolescence. He now thought of this place, which in those
days he called The Garden, as the graveyard of his
youth—a vacant, desolate land where he'd been forced
to learn to grow up. The only traces of it he had left

were a few objects that served as permanent testimony
to his childhood, marks of his memory: a Russian edition of Pushkin's *Tales of the Late Ivan Petrovich
Belkin*, a Daumier lithograph, a plaster bust of a Bohe-
mian woman, his grandfather's cane, Volumes 1 and 6
of the 1923 edition of the *Complete Works* of Gustave
Flaubert, and his first camera, a 1936 Leica.

Then there were the records and tapes that
would later be stolen, replaced, given away, and replaced again, always by the same artists: Schnabel,
Kleiber, and the Vegh Quartet for Beethoven, Bach by
Menuhin and Max van Egmond, Bartók by Fritz
Reiner, Callas for Mozart and Verdi, Julius Katchen
for Brahms, and Stravinsky by himself. He never did
manage to find an interpretation of Beethoven's Opus
26 by Wanda Landowska (he especially liked the third
movement, *Marcia funebre sulla morte d'un eroe)*,
though he looked for it everywhere.

At the time he met the girl, he had cut himself
off from his family. He'd just bought a turntable for
the records, and he listened to music while reading
screenplays and books on film history. His life was
replete with futile, silent rebellions.

$\mathcal{T}$hat first evening after he'd walked her home, he opened the gate of The Garden very carefully and tiptoed under the second-story windows, crouching to elude the widow's chatty curiosity.

He found the light on in his room. A girl named Isabelle was sitting on the bed waiting for him. She had very light straight blond hair with bangs and an ivory complexion. Her jet-black gaze seemed even darker against the pallor of her face. Her eyes were unusually animated, expressing flashes of pleasure and pain that never seemed to touch the mouth, smile, or cheekbones.

That night her eyes said expectation. But he didn't know that. He stood in the middle of the room, assailed by contradictory thoughts. He would have preferred to have been left alone with the girl from the café until he fell asleep.

He took off his coat. When he turned around he saw that Isabelle had stretched out on the bed. She lay on her back and looked at him.

"I'd like to sleep with you," she said. "It'll be my first time."

She was smoking a cigarette. Everyone smoked during their adolescence. Everyone but him.

"Since it's the first time, I'd like it to be you," she added.

Had she put it differently, had she said something like, "I'd like you to be the first one," had she shown any hint of warmth or tenderness, he might have suggested another day and another place—in short, another man. But the cold crudeness of the request seemed perfectly suited to what he was able to give that evening, so he went to the bed. There was no love between them, just a fleeting tenderness, as was so often the case with girls that age. When he took Isabelle in his arms, the girl from the café slipped away, with exquisite courtesy.

The next day she walked over to his table, pushed the chessboard aside, and said, "There's something important we forgot to tell each other yesterday."

He waited.

"You know what it is?"

He shook his head.

"Think about it."

She had on a white shift, a faux pearl necklace, and enamel earrings.

"You don't see it?"

He knew very well what it was they hadn't told each other, but he wanted her to rectify the omission. He'd thought about it all night. So had she. Later they both admitted they enjoyed the speculation. It allowed them to dream a little.

"I think yours is probably very short," he said, leaning forward slightly. "Short and sweet. Something like Masha. Or maybe Tanya."

"And yours is hyphenated."

They spent a long time guessing, until finally she had to go home.

"It's Anna," she said as she stood up.

"I'm Luca," he replied.

Luca gazed at the slumbering countryside beyond the frosted windows. He'd been this way many times before. He didn't recognize the places, but the train was the same. Just like the one he'd taken that first time, when he was working on that first script.

He was twenty-two and was coming from Leningrad. At the station in Moscow he got off and bought a spiral notebook. Back in his compartment he drew the curtains, rested the notebook on the mahogany tray in front of him, and started to write.

He remembered that train well, for it was just like this one. An ancient Russian train with copper siding, as slow as in olden days, with springs that creaked as it rolled along the rails. He crossed landscapes just like the ones that drifted now past the window. Tumbledown cottages, a few fields, dark shadows of crumbling buildings.

Luca had written and directed nine films since then, but none was as dear to him as that first one, the one he'd never made. But now he knew he would, because when he pictured the women in his life, when he imagined a female silhouette leaning over Pushkin's shoulder as he wrote, it was the girl he saw in his mind's eye. It was Anna who held out her hand to him.

And Luca took it.

He remembered the question she'd asked on the seventh day. Why *Luca?* He didn't want to tell her yet. They didn't know each other well enough. He was in no mood to unveil his legends, but she insisted. She was sitting on a log in the Saint-Germain-en-Laye forest. He was taking pictures of her with his Leica. The play of the sunlight on her pupils gave her eyes a stunningly vivid energy. Luca wanted to capture that look. "Don't move," he said. "Whatever you do, don't move!"

He shot the picture.

"You didn't answer me," Anna said.

He put in a new roll of film.

"My grandfather was Russian and Romanian. From Bessarabia, a province wedged between those two countries."

"I've been there," Anna said.

He wanted to leave it at that, but she kept staring at him, waiting for more, so he went on. He told her his grandfather had emigrated to France before the war and enlisted in the International Brigades in Spain. In 1937 his best friend was killed before his very eyes, on the Aragon front. The friend was Romanian. His name was Luca Klein.

She didn't ask anything else, and Luca could have gone on shooting in silence. Instead he hefted the camera and said, "This Leica belonged to Klein."

He didn't tell her the rest, didn't tell her that in a hidden corner of his bookshelf was a family photo he carried with him everywhere. It showed five people sitting on the balustrade of a house. The house was in Kishinev, capital of Bessarabia, and the five people, from left to right, were Luca's grandfather, his great-grandfather, and his grandfather's sister, mother, and brother. All five are staring into the camera with sweet serenity. And today all five are dead.

When he looked at that picture, Luca often tried to imagine how frozen with fear those sweet and peaceful faces must have been a few years later, when Nazis with machine guns drove their prisoners to the Dniester before hurling them into the river's dark waters. But he had never been able to imagine death's shadow falling over eyes that seemed so alive.

In his mind the annihilation of the family he never knew was the embodiment of absolute savagery. The image of his relatives being cast into the swirl of water and bullets would stay with him all his life. The tragedy he would forever bear within himself culminated on that bridge over the Dniester ten years before his birth. Luca's family had been wiped out. Its history now lived in him alone. He thought of himself as the last survivor.

He didn't say this to Anna. Not that day or later. It made him feel awkward, reticent. He didn't enjoy explaining himself.

He looked at her through the camera's viewfinder. She had a narrow waist, delicate ankles. She shifted her position as the sun moved, and finally, when dusk fell, her pupils turned jet black, her irises flecked with bronze just the way he wanted.

"I'll give you the best print," he said. "We'll keep just the one, and I'll destroy the negatives."

She didn't want that. "No," she said. "You keep them all, forever."

He felt like taking her in his arms, but he didn't.

It was like a word he didn't allow himself to say. Something drove him toward her, but he fought it. He was afraid she'd be terrified, afraid she would say, "All you want is to sleep with me."

But since that wasn't all he wanted, he was patient. He wanted her to make the first move. The inner violence that shook him now he had never felt for anyone else.

They saw each other every day, but still he didn't really feel he knew her. He found himself unable to picture her face exactly when he wasn't with her. He could visualize her shape, her smile, her eyes, and the way she moved, but the features were less distinct than her expressions. All he knew of her was what she gave him, and that was just what charmed him. It was as if a language of their own were slowly flowering between them. As he waited for her in the back room of the café each evening, he was afraid of being less dazzled than he'd been the day or the moment before, when he was alone with a wondrous abstraction.

But she always surprised him. She did her hair in different ways—sometimes braids, sometimes a pony tail, sometimes a bun. One day she would show up in a dark suit, the next in jeans and a shaggy sweater like the other students. The sweater was usually faded, either pink or mauve, often with those little holes in the back or front that were so fashionable at the time.

She offered him different facets of herself, and he admired them all. It made her seem unpredictable, and therefore free.

She took him on endless walks. "That's what we do in Leningrad," she said. "Lovers spend hours walking along the river and in the parks."

When she talked about Leningrad, which she called "Peter," she made it sound like the flowered wallpaper of a room she'd never lived in. She compressed space to the dimensions of her memories, which stretched from the seaside station to the Kazan Cathedral. She told him that the wind blowing past the golden steeples smelled of seaweed and the ocean, that every morning she would sit at the window of the little room she shared with other children and watch the spire of the Admiralty pierce the gloomy clouds. In France she was always astonished when she awoke all alone in a room tinged with pink. In spring, if the window was open, she sometimes mistook the distant peak of the Eiffel Tower for the Admiralty. But the illusion didn't last. And eventually she forgot the smell of the sea.

She told him she was born on March 5, 1953, a day when sirens wailed in factories and aboard ships, and gongs and bells rang out, and there was cannon and rifle fire in all the towns and all the cities throughout the land, from the Gulf of Finland to the Bering Strait. "But it wasn't for me. It was for Stalin. That was the day he died, making room for me."

She told him it was her father who came home with the news of Stalin's death, just a few hours before they left their communal apartment on the Nevski Prospekt for the hospital. She said her mother had told her the story a hundred times. Her father had written it down, and she asked Luca to take notes as she told it to him, so he would remember it in case he ever decided to use it in a film. She said that, if he did, the opening shot should be a pan of the Peter and Paul Fortress, with the opening lines of Osip Mandelstam's poem "Leningrad" superimposed in black letters:

> *I returned to the town I knew so well, to the sobs*
> *And the ganglia of childhood, to the veins*
>   *beneath the skin.*

She said her mother was stretched out on the bed, the three other tenants standing by. She had her hands on her belly. Her hair was woven into a braid that formed a halo above her face. The light from the flame of a large candle glinted on her eyes and mouth, glittering black eyes and lips of great purity, one of them bearing a tiny birthmark, like a delicate stain.

Her mother looked over at the door, which opened to reveal a tall, thin man—Anna's father. He wore a heavy fur coat, its collar flecked with frost. He came in, closed the door behind him, and went to the bed, his face gleaming with ineffable happiness. He leaned over his wife and kissed her forehead, her lips, her hands. Then he turned to the others and said, "The rat is gone. Dead as a doornail."

They stood and hugged one another. Someone went to the sink, took five glasses, and filled them with water. There were silent toasts. They were all overcome.

She said her mother left Sveko Hospital on the day of Stalin's funeral, her laughter mingling with the official dirge. Just as she was opening the door to their Leningrad apartment, a cohort of bemedaled dignitaries stood in Moscow's Red Square—Khrushchev, Beria, Malenkov, Bulganin—and saluted the defunct

Master's mummified remains. The masses were be-
reaved. But Anna had come into the world.

She said that from the day she was born her
parents were determined that her path would diverge
from theirs and carry her back to the world her
mother had lost. Her story, she said, was inseparable
from her mother's. Luca would never understand her
until he knew her parents' fate.

Her mother was born in Marseilles. Her mother's
parents were Armenians who emigrated to France after the massacre of the community by the Turks. But
after the war they were seduced by the siren calls of
Stalingrad and Yalta, Thorez and Mikoyan. One fine
day they set out for Soviet Armenia aboard a lovely
white ship whose passengers gathered on the deck to
greet them with cries of "Long live the USSR! Long
live the Father of Peoples!"

She said it was on the coast of the Black Sea that
her mother suddenly realized what the Soviet paradise
would be like. The immigrants had been given bread,
and when they cast it symbolically on the waters, fish-
ermen rowed frantically to pluck it from the sea. Fifteen years later her mother continued to marvel: "It
was soaked in sea water and still they gobbled it up!"

Her grandparents did all they could to get back
to France. They never made it. Neither did her
mother. Her parents met at the headquarters of the

Writers' Union in Moscow. She was a translator; he had just finished college. He had published a few poems and was about to leave for Leningrad, where he would teach philosophy at the university. They decided to get married there.

She said her first memory dated from when she was four. She was drawing on brown wrapping paper with a piece of coal. Her mother looked at the drawing and asked what it was. "A horse," the little girl said. "Do you know how to say *horse* in French?" the mother asked. *"Cheval,"* Anna replied. "Good. And *giraffe?"* She knew that too.

"I also knew how to say *bus, rabbit, princess,* and *potato.* And later *plane, trip, Champs-Élysées, Paris,* and *au revoir.* My parents brought me up to believe I'd get out. They loved me too much to share me. They wanted a little girl, not a little Soviet girl, if you know what I mean."

Every Sunday her mother would take her to the base of the Alexander Column at Palace Square, where they would lie in wait for French tourists and walk alongside them, listening to them talk. Often they would offer their services as guides—not for money, but to hear words the little girl would later write down on the colored blocks her father had made for her.

She said the first years of her life were probably the happiest. She remembered the swings in the Summer Gardens, a mauve dress her mother made for her, hopscotch games in the courtyard where a carpenter worked. She was a little girl then, still a child.

In 1958 her father was expelled from the Writers' Union for publicly supporting Boris Pasternak, who had just won the Nobel Prize. Any writer or poet not recognized by the union was considered a parasite. That was the official term: parasite. No one would publish anything her father wrote anymore; even the newspapers were closed to him. Instead he would recite poems for small audiences in the Mayakovsky Library and later at Gorky House. Her mother would sit in the back row. The union had withdrawn her translations from circulation. She always wore an old fur coat, and Anna would fall asleep in her arms.

Her father was fired from the university. He was out of work for a year, then found a job as a warehouse packer. Later he laid pipe and ran a mechanical shovel. His blue worker's uniforms were coarser than his professor's suits. The family lived on bread and potatoes, but she didn't miss meat. It was already in such short supply, she'd forgotten it.

She said she remembered a classroom scene when she was eight. There was a portrait of Lenin on the wall. Pupils were assigned to make drawings of the first man in space. Anna drew a face with vacant eye sockets. The teacher glanced at her drawing, tore it up, and told her to do another one. Anna put down her pencils and walked out. That night her father scolded her, and as she wept in her room he took her in his arms and begged her never to call attention to herself. That was when she first understood her father's tragedy: he would punish her as a child so the Soviet state wouldn't punish her later, preventing her from leaving because of some sin committed in her youth. "He traced out my destiny from the day I was born," she said. "It was a line as straight as the Bolshoi Prospekt, from Leningrad to Paris, with the briefest possible stopover at the Foreign Languages Institute."

She also said: "Maybe it was because I had to learn to make mischief in silence, but ever since that day I've made my drawings illegible. Because even if I wasn't supposed to, it was fun to poke out Yuri Gagarin's eyes."

She said she remembered the room she shared with another little girl and two boys who slept head to foot. Her bed was painted pink and decorated with decals of flowers and little animals. There was a celluloid doll on a shelf, a few picture books, a pair of broken castanets, a hoop, and a tiny white lace-up shoe.

Most of all she remembered that the walls were too thin and that she was always afraid when she heard moans and sighs coming from the next room. She would plug up her ears, roll over, and pull the covers over her head. Later she came to understand what those noises were.

She said her parents invited a few classmates over for her tenth birthday. It was her first party. The children sat at a round table, drinking water through straws made of macaroni.

That was the day her father gave her a framed print of a portrait of a woman by Modigliani. Her father leaned the picture against a wall and said, "Her name is Anna Akhmatova. Can you say that?"

Anna hesitated for a moment and then repeated, "Anna Akhmatova."

"Again."

"Anna Akhmatova, Anna Akhmatova, Anna Akhmatova."

"Her name is the first of her poems," her father said. "She's a woman who's suffered a lot."

Anna went to the picture. Her fingers brushed the poet's face. "She's beautiful," she whispered.

She said she remembered her last meeting of the Young Communist League. The audience was listening to an adolescent older than the others. He was perched on a dais.

"Do you know why the sun doesn't shine at night?" he asked.

No one answered.

"Because," he went on, "the enemies of our people turn it off to stop us from building communism."

The audience burst out laughing. The young man pounded his fist on the table several times. The crowd fell silent. Then he continued: "What is the main role of the Supreme Soviet?"

No one answered.

"The main role of the Supreme Soviet is to eliminate the rich!"

Anna stood up in the back of the hall, pointed at the dais, and exclaimed, "Comrade, it is not the rich who must be eliminated, but the poor!"

She was afraid she'd made a horrible blunder. She thought of her father. But the crowd broke into applause.

A year later she had a boyfriend. One evening he came to pick her up at the institute with a guitar slung over his shoulder. He was a musician. He kissed her on both cheeks, took her by the waist, and led her to the sidewalk. She didn't want him to hold her like that. She twisted free. He took her hand.

"Not my hand!" she snapped.

"Then what?"

"Nothing."

They walked to the headquarters of the Union of Composers, where the food was good. The boyfriend treated her to some cake. Musicians had certain privileges, he explained. Since their works weren't published, they were not considered dangerous.

"That's why they shoot writers," he said, "but not musicians or painters."

"But what if some apparatchik hears your songs?" Anna asked.

"Well," the young man replied, "since I want to keep my privileges, I write music without lyrics."

He put his arms around her. She tried to wriggle away. "You know how a policeman opens a jar of preserves?" the young man asked.

Anna shook her head.

"He knocks on the lid."

She laughed.

"You know how a policeman makes sure a box of matches isn't empty?"

"No."

"He shakes his head."

She laughed again. The young man took the opportunity to put his mouth on hers. She struggled a little but then gave in. She kept her eyes open. It was her first kiss.

She said she remembered a day in August. She was sitting at the kitchen table, drawing. Her father was keeping an eye on the samovar. The radio was on. Suddenly there was martial music, then an announcer's voice. Her father turned up the volume; her mother came into the room; Anna looked up from her drawing. She said she would never forget the announcer's words: "This morning, acting under the auspices of the Warsaw Pact, armed forces of brother countries entered Czechoslovakia."

She scribbled frantically all over her sheet of paper, crumpled it up, and threw it across the room. She looked up at her mother and father and said, "I'm glad *I* don't have a brother."

She said she remembered the last day, that horrible last day. It had snowed all morning. Everyone pretended they'd slept well. They all said "Good morning" and "Gee, it's cold" with happy smiles. There was a brioche on the kitchen table. She'd never tasted one before. She declared that it was excellent and that she would send some from Paris, but she never did. She said they acted as though it were an ordinary morning that would be followed by an ordinary afternoon, evening, and night, with a yesterday and a tomorrow just like any other day. Two suitcases stood in a corner. Her father handed her some official papers as though they were nothing at all. Her mother gave her her coat, as if the idea had just occurred to her, but the coat had been cleaned and brushed, all the buttons were new, and it was that coat and not another. She said they finally hurried out, because they felt smothered by the familiar setting. The other tenants offered to treat them to a taxi, but they refused. They knew it would take longer by trolley bus.

On the way they talked about the beauty of the city she was now leaving. When she came back it would be summer. Birds, tranquillity, reunion. But they knew that summer would dawn without her. No birds, tranquillity, or reunion for her. This was a city founded on death and the knout, built on the bones of peasant founders who dropped from exhaustion and were drowned in the bogs. They knew she was leaving for a long time, perhaps for good.

A few miles from the airport a pain shot through her from groin to solar plexus. She tried to rise from her seat but fell back down. "It felt like my legs were cut off," she said. She said she would feel like that for the rest of her life, defenseless whenever the threat of abandonment loomed. She said she could always detect the signs—a look, an expression, a gesture, a word—by their physical effects on her body.

Her last view of Leningrad was the airport waiting room. People scurried back and forth, lugging bulging suitcases and cardboard boxes tied with cord.

She looked back several times as she walked across the tarmac to a stairway leading to a plane. She said she felt torn in half. She was in tears; she wanted to keep on pretending but didn't have the strength.

Her mother and father were pressed against a filthy partition with a group of other people, struggling to keep her in sight as long as possible, as far as possible. She would always remember how they looked: all dressed up, their shoes shined, her mother wearing more makeup than usual, her father carefully shaved, both standing behind the grill, erect and dignified but broken and ravaged, putting up the best possible front for their little girl, holding out the smiles and ruffles of grand days to come, days free of lies.

Sometimes when she thought of her parents she felt afraid and wanted to see them again. "I'm afraid and I want to see them again," she repeated. Then she fell silent. She put her head on his shoulder and closed her eyes, as though setting down a weight too heavy to bear. Luca said nothing. He took her hand. He felt an almost imperceptible resistance, but eventually she yielded, and he put her hand into his own pocket. He wished it could stay there forever and ever.

She talked more about Leningrad, telling him
about the Nevsky Prospekt with its overhanging electric grid for the tramways and about the cruiser *Au-
rora*, with its three smokestacks and giant cannon,
which fired the blanks that signaled the October
Revolution in 1917. She said she still wasn't used to
the colors, smells, and architecture of the cities of
Western Europe and that in her memory Peter was
like an Italian palace overlooking the Great North. Its
fog always seemed so light, and she would never read

with as much joy as she did under the pink-tinged sky during the white nights of June.

They walked along the Seine—"What a narrow river!"—down streets bordered by colorless facades. She told him she wanted to see London and the Thames, Vienna and the Danube, Rome and the Tiber. Luca realized that she was seeking illusory reflections of the pastel tints—sea green, ocher, pale yellow—that soothed her childhood and adolescence. He also realized that emigrating had been like being wrenched away and drowned. She had been taken from her parents and plunged into a world of which she knew nothing but the language. Even her uncle and aunt were strangers to her. "He's a merchant and she's a housewife. My father was a working-class writer, my mother a teacher. It's a big change."

Last of all he realized that a single year had not been enough to free her from the contradictory memories of a city whose physical beauty harbored a secret, ineluctable harshness, like the frigid interiors that lurked behind the soft, pastel facades. Luca saw the signs and thought of them as wounds. The worst was probably Anna's refusal to address him by the familiar *tu*, which made him unsure of what to call her. Sometimes he said *vous*, sometimes *tu*, depending on the moment. He would take her by the arm, the hand, the neck, and still she called him *vous*. She explained in her own defense that everyone in Russia used the equivalent of *tu*—at school, in the street, when speaking to Party members. She had come to see it as a kind of compulsory handshake that she preferred to avoid now that she had the choice.

She couldn't abide acts she considered inappropriate, like kissing in the street. When she saw couples embracing in public places, she would stare with dread-tinged astonishment. When Luca pulled her close, she would put her fists against his chest to push him back, glancing around to see if anyone was watching. "People will see us, a cop will come." But people here weren't like people there, and cops were rare.

She was often unpredictably vivacious, charmingly extravagant and whimsical. But sometimes she was disconcertingly solemn. She worked on her drawings with a gravity he had never seen. She drew constantly, keeping a sketchbook in her purse and taking it out at any moment, in cafés, on the bus, even during intermissions at the movies. She drew abstract figures whose faces seemed unfinished and whose posture—the curve of an arm, the angle of a hand—seemed to express what the features concealed: mendacity, anger, vanity, generosity. The whole multicolored palette of character.

Anna told him she had embarked on a work that would take a lifetime. "It's going to be a fresco portraying the entire human race. I started very early and I'll finish very late."

She added that she had worked on her project continually in the city where she grew up, a place she once loved but now hated because her parents were trapped there. She saw her drawing not as a talent but as a way of defining and expressing herself. Even as a child, she liked herself only when she was applying her colors to a piece of paper. She believed it was all she had to offer: "Without my pencils I wouldn't exist. I wouldn't matter."

Then she shook her head and added, with that little-girl solemnity: "The only thing I really know about myself is that I draw to survive."

One evening about two weeks after they met they saw an unchained Solex moped leaning against the trunk of a tree near the café.

They had almost reached the top of the slope leading to her uncle and aunt's house when suddenly she stopped and turned to Luca with a look so lost and disconsolate that he took his hand out of his pocket and stroked her cheek, slipping his fingers under her hair and softly caressing the nape of her neck.

"I forgot my Solex!" she murmured.

He stared at her, nonplussed.

"I left it at the café."

"A Solex?"

She nodded, looking into his eyes.

"I didn't know you had a Solex."

"I do."

Luca was dumbfounded. "You have a Solex?" he repeated.

She took a step backward, anger glinting in her eyes. Her hands closed into fists.

He moved his arm and accidentally dropped the chess set, spilling the pieces onto the ground. When they had gathered them up in the darkening dusk, they turned back down the path, walking one behind the other, paying no attention to passing cars.

The Solex was still there when they got to the café. Luca connected the motor, pushed the starter lever, and jumped on. He braked, and she climbed on behind him, sitting astride the baggage carrier. She held the chess set under her coat. He pedaled to build up speed for the upward slope. Anna held onto his waist. He pedaled hard, thinking about how she was sitting there behind him with her fingers on his hips, and he decided that if he could make it to the top of the slope without putting his foot down, she would be his forever.

"Faster!" she shouted.

She tried to wish herself lighter. The motor labored, Luca was drenched in sweat. Anna never took her hands off his hips. He stood on the pedals, and the higher they climbed, the more frantically he pedaled. They were both silent now, grimly yearning for the peak of the path. When they finally pulled up in front of the residence for mid-level managers, she jumped off and screamed, "Turn it off, turn it off!"

He turned it off. She stood in front of the machine, sporting a slightly clownish pout. "It's not my Solex," she said.

He looked at her, as nonplussed as before.

"We stole it. I never had a Solex. It was a bet I made."

Luca tried to catch his breath.

"A bet with myself. But I can't tell you what it was."

He said nothing. He waited a moment, turned the Solex to face downhill, and started off. The engine caught. Anna watched him roll away. She thought he was angry with her, but she didn't care about that, because she'd won her bet: he would be the love of her life. But Luca wasn't angry. He traveled a few yards, spun so sharply that the rear wheel skidded, and rode back to Anna, pulling up in front of her.

"Go on home now," he said.

"What about the Solex?"

"Let's keep it."

She didn't budge.

"We'll keep it," he repeated. "From now on let's consider it ours."

Twenty years later he still remembered that Solex. It was black, with a rectangular headlight and a red stripe on the fender. You started it by pushing it and stopped it with a little gray lever on the handlebars, near the handbrake for the front wheel, which acted as an accelerator when you released it. It wasn't the first one Luca had stolen. He'd once taken one from the parking lot of the residence for mid-level managers. Maybe that was why he handled the machine with such unparalleled skill. Not that his top speed was any better than anyone else's, but over long distances he was unbeatable—even with Anna perched behind him, clinging to his waist or riding sidesaddle. If he lost ground on the straightaway, he regained it on the curves, negotiating turns like no one else, sticking his foot out to prevent the engine from being dislodged by the bouncing front wheel, which bore the motor's weight. He was fearless. Luca and Anna laughingly went where friends slowed down to preserve a precarious balance.

The Solex meant a lot in their life, for it was the first thing they owned in common and the first to be taken from them. Luca could always pick out the strange crackling sound of a moped amid the din of a hundred other engines. Years later he would come to hate that sound; whenever he heard it he would also hear Anna's laugh and feel her hands around his waist, and however unlikely or impossible it was, he would turn to see who the rider was, looking to see if she was dark, and if her hair streamed behind her like the wake of an undying image.

It was never her.

It was always her.

He remembered it all. The way he waited for her in the morning at the green door, and she'd come out not yet completely awake, eyes still puffy with sleep, books bound by the crossed elastic straps, and say, "Hi, Luca," and climb onto the baggage carrier.

The way she held her legs out in front of her or folded back as she rode, her legs bare, without tights or stockings, the way she spoke loud enough for him to hear above the rush of the wind and the noise of the motor.

The way she thumbed her nose at bad drivers or yelled, "I can't swim!" when they went through puddles or "You broke my back!" when he failed to avoid a pothole.

The way she pedaled frantically to come out of a skid while he inadvertently tilted the bike off balance by lifting his butt off the hooks of the baggage carrier, trying to find a more comfortable position.

He remembered how they zigzagged through traffic, one laughing, the other's knuckles white on the handlebars.

And how they sped through the rain, pressing hard on the lever of the motor to keep it against the wheel.

And how they turned off the engine to pick up speed going downhill.

He remembered the day they had a plate made with their names on it and screwed it to the handlebars.

And the day they decided to call the Solex Dubrovsky, and she gave him Pushkin to read.

And the day she was expecting a phone call from her parents and asked him to call her late, and Luca phoned from a booth at one in the morning and didn't hang up till three, and he felt like he was repairing something that absence had broken.

And the day she came to his place for the first time and sat on the leather ottoman like a proper guest, and he tried to find a way not to act as he did with all the others all the other times, and she realized it and stood up and left. He caught up with her in the garden and they went through the gate together and she slipped her hand under his arm, but they were sad. They loved that sadness.

And the day they finally kissed, three weeks after they met in the back room of the café.

They were on the moped, between Louveciennes and Port-Marly, on their way back from a walk in the woods. The autumn colors were fading into winter, the browns, ochers, and moist blacks turning pale and dirty. She'd let him hold her hand, and they'd walked in complete silence.

Anna decided to drive home. He sat behind her, fingers gripping the seat. The road was straight, and then there was a very gentle curve. Anna pulled over, stopped, and got off. Luca stood astride the Solex, his feet wide apart.

She put her hands on his cheeks, stared deep into his eyes with that blue, blue gaze, and her lips came near, and they kissed, with their eyes closed, breathing each other in, trying to convey with that kiss what they both thought would never again exist with anyone else, she leaning slightly toward him, he all tense, hands on his hips, like a cloud on the metal baggage carrier.

She drew away from him and climbed back onto the Solex, and they rode in silence toward the Seine, the engine off.

Neither of them spoke a word until they got to her place. Even there, at the foot of the building where her aunt and uncle lived, they said nothing. She got off, he took the handlebars, and they parted in the usual way. This time, though, he waited for her to wave to him from her window before heading home.

⌒

*A*nd the day they first said they loved each other.

It was the Thursday before Christmas.

They were at one of the ponds of Vésinet. The

water was a dull blue-green. A few water lilies were scattered near the bank. Anna crouched near the water's edge and called to the frogs. Luca stood behind her, watching his beloved. Her long, pale gray socks with green edging were pulled up over faded jeans. She wore the mohair sweater she'd had on that first time, and a hooded, thick wool jacket frayed at the elbows.

She put a finger to her lips and motioned him to come over. He knelt beside her. She pointed to a gray spot on a green spot: a frog perched on a lily pad. He was less enthralled by the frog and the plant than he was by Anna's tender expression, by how touched she was by those two little things he pretended to be interested in. She was moved by nature's beauty, he by how innocent and enchanted she looked, one knee to the ground, one hand pointing toward the water.

When the frog leaped into the mud, he put his arms around her, kissed the hollow of her ear, and whispered, "I love you, Anna, I love you."

She pulled away from him, looked at him with her big blue eyes, and said, "I love you too. Yes, I love you too." And they ran along the bank of the pond, hand in hand, laughing.

It was the first time Luca had ever said that to a woman. And the first time anyone had ever said it to him. When he looked back on it now, remembering the sound of Anna's voice, so solemn yet so alive, he felt like standing up and striding back to the dining car, hoping to recapture what he merely dreamed of here.

But he didn't.

O*ne evening* they ran into Isabelle in the street in front of The Garden. The girls sized each other up with a quick, grim look before a single word was spoken.

Awkward and embarrassed, Luca introduced them. Anna laughed at his clumsiness. Isabelle said, "You might at least give me a ring once in a while." He promised he would, but he didn't mean it.

"You made love with her," Anna murmured when they were alone.

That was how she put it: "You made love." She didn't say, "You slept with her." She wouldn't. She was always modest when that subject came up, as though the lack of coarseness of simple words would lend poetry to an act that frightened her. She spoke of love as people sometimes do at that age: thinking of deathless promises and happy futures more than the mere joining of bodies.

"You made love with her. And if you made love with her, there were probably others as well. We're not the same."

Until the moment they ran into Isabelle, she never wanted to, as she made perfectly clear without ever actually saying so. She let him touch her face, her neck, her shoulders, but no more. He was never allowed to kiss her ears, or to slip his hand under the strap of her bra, or to hold her for very long. He could put his hand on her back—sometimes even her lower back—but never lower than that, and never ever in front.

A few days later she said, "I don't really want to, but I'm curious."

The following Thursday, at Luca's, she took a deep breath, closed her eyes, and deliberately placed his hand on her breast, the left breast, over the heart. "It's a little scary," she commented, "but not too unpleasant."

After that she had terrible trouble getting him to understand that this was a limit not to be transgressed. When he tried, she protested. "That's not how it works, you know. Just because I gave you a breast doesn't mean you can have everything."

But since she didn't want to lose him, she let him go a little further, swearing all the while that no, she would never go all the way.

Her breast was a tender, tiny bulge, with nipples like a young boy's. She was astonished when they swelled gently under his touch. "My breasts get bigger between your fingers," she said. "You know how to do things. Not that it matters, but where did you learn how to do that?"

She said she wasn't built as well as Isabelle, and he assured her she had the world's most beautiful chest. She shrugged, but she was delighted. She relaxed under his touch, and the great Thursday afternoon games began.

They kissed passionately and constantly. Luca was patient, hoping that desire, languor, and forgetfulness would work their magic. He felt guilty in spite of himself, but he never gave up trying to encroach on the forbidden, southern zone. He would let his hand linger on her breast, first above her lace bra and later underneath it, then he would slide it slightly lower and pretend to stop, waiting for Anna to relax before spreading his fingers, thumb extended upward to reassure her, little finger as low as possible, tempting fate.

At that point Anna would break off the kiss, tug the alien hand higher, and offer him her mouth again. Luca would wait a good fifteen minutes before trying again, the same thing but slower, as if by chance.

The very first time was at The Garden one Thursday afternoon. She waited absolutely motionless as he unbuttoned her dress, lying on her back, staring at a point on the ceiling, a bewildered look in her eyes. Luca took her clothes off with great patience, caressing her face, constantly reassuring her in word and gesture.

He remembered that she barely moved, and that when he withdrew from her she was still looking up at the ceiling, lips trembling slightly, weeping in silence.

He wasn't sure whether they were tears of pain, emotion, or a vague sense of humiliation of which he was the cause and which aroused in him a guilt he had never felt with Isabelle or anyone else.

Finally she took his hand, her tears dried, and she stood up brusquely. They never talked about that first time. He vividly recalled the gesture she made when climbing astride the Solex: a scissor-like movement, a sway of the hips, a quick spin, the sweep of a leg. It was exactly the reverse of the gesture she made when she let herself go. Luca saw it as a magic trick.

After that first time they spent many afternoons in bed in The Garden. She now yielded to his touch without too much reluctance. When he put his hand on her breast, she would sigh, "Again?" in polite exasperation, and sometimes she would let him caress her shoulder, her back, her belly. But not always. There were times when she gently disentangled herself and said, "Not today," holding herself so tightly against him as to keep him prisoner.

She never learned how to fully abandon herself to the slow onslaught of desire, or how to take Luca's clothes off, or how to let him undress her in the serene haste of love's motions. She would close her eyes, hold her arms at her sides, clench her fists, and sink into herself. She took no initiative, never caressed him. Afterward she would curl up and huddle against him, her knees against his torso. At moments like those, it seemed to Luca that she betrayed a vulnerability that reminded him of how she looked when she tilted her neck back with that deep, sad sigh.

What he didn't know was that what he took to be modesty, fear, and embarrassment were in fact scars of her childhood, when Anna lay in her room and heard noises and moans from behind the wooden partition (sounds that must have been made by the tenants who shared the communal apartment and never ever by her parents) and when, having no idea what those noises meant, she imagined lurking ghosts, trolls, and monsters, finally falling asleep, engulfed in her nightmares.

Years later Luca would remember her fears, secrets, and frailties. He would recall that she was tender though not especially sensual, rarely speaking of such things, which were not an essential language between them. He remembered her as an inexperienced adolescent, charming and slightly intimidated, marked by the peculiarities of the age, when you write the word "love" with a capital L. Maybe he was fooling himself, but when he thought about their Thursday afternoons in his room in The Garden, he felt a twinge of melancholy—not so much the kind inevitably brought by the passage of time, but the subtle, fragile pain of irrevocable loss.

It was the dead of night when the train pulled into Poznań. Disembarking passengers made their way down the corridor. Luca lay on his bunk and watched sweepers working on the platform. A raspy voice announced that the train would stop for two minutes. A vague fear suddenly came over him. He wondered whether she would get off, and whether he would follow her if she did. Finally he had to know. He lowered the window and leaned out. Three passengers made their way toward the stairs. The train was curved in a wide arc. The cars were green, with yellow bands just below the roofs. There was writing in Cyrillic letters on the bands.

A man got off not far away. He put his suitcase down, turned, and extended his hand. Luca saw another hand, gloved he thought, and then a woman joined the man on the platform. The man picked up the suitcase and the couple disappeared in the mist.

He wondered if she was traveling alone and under what name. He wondered in which European city they would separate, and whether they would meet again in the dining car or somewhere else. Would she recognize him if they did?

He saw a female silhouette in the distance, walking away from the train. A motorized cart approached from the opposite direction. He leaned out a little further. The frigid air caught him full in the face. He leaned further out, and the train gave a soft jolt. The woman wore a long white fur coat. She carried a traveling bag in her right hand. Her face was concealed by the night shadows.

The train began to pick up speed. Luca braced himself on the window ledge with both hands. Half his torso hung outside the car. A fraction of a second before he passed her, the woman veered to her right to let the cart pass. Luca never saw her face. He tried to contain himself, but as the train accelerated, he called out, "Mademoiselle!"

The cart blocked his view. He craned his neck desperately, and his last sight of Poznań station was of a railroad employee in a red cap facing him, then turning to look back before being engulfed by the distance and the fog.

He closed the window and sat down on the lower berth. The night light cast a pale glow that glinted softly on the copper sink and the wall paneling. He had chosen to travel on this superannuated Russian luxury train because he thought it would give him time to relax and get some work done. He enjoyed isolating himself in sealed places where nothing and no one could disturb him. This journey was supposed to have been different. He'd planned to work on the notes he'd taken in St. Petersburg. He wanted to ponder the locations he'd scouted for his film, compare photographs of houses, landscapes, actresses. But it didn't work out that way. He'd gone to the dining car, and that was that. His mind was somewhere else now. It would stay there.

He opened the door to the compartment and went into the deserted corridor. Through the windows across the aisle he saw trees rushing by, then the dark mass of a farm and the headlights of a car stopped at a railroad crossing. The train picked up speed again, plunging into the shapeless night.

He walked up the corridor, his shoes sinking into thick carpeting whose pattern he couldn't make out. The compartments were all shielded by drawn curtains, the impeccable order concealing the extraordinary release of sleep. He pictured the girl behind one of these darkened windows, wearing a long nightgown with lace trim, probably lying on her side, breathing softly, one hand under her cheek, the other stretched out along her body, palm open. Luca imagined opening the door, catching her at that vulnerable, intimate moment when your eyes first open on a new day. He would stand in the doorway, and she would look at him first with the helpless glance of fresh awakening and then with dawning incredulity, confusion, joy, and perhaps anger as well.

The conductor stood at the far end of the third car, forehead pressed against the glass, staring out into the night. Luca cleared his throat and said, *"Bon jour."* The conductor answered, *"Bon soir."*

"You're French?"

Luca nodded. The conductor was a young man

in a dark uniform. He held his cap in his hand. His trousers were too big and too long for him. They swam on his thighs and legs.

"You're not sleeping?" Luca asked.

"Yes, I am. As you can see, I'm asleep. I often sleep standing up and talk at the same time. Please don't wake me."

Luca didn't know what to say. What he wanted to ask was as incongruous as the answer he'd just gotten to what was admittedly a stupid question.

The conductor put both hands on the guardrail and continued to stare out the window. Luca looked too. There were low hills in the distance, their crests streaked by moonlight.

They stood in silence for long moments. Luca felt a growing unease. As the train rounded a broad curve, the man said, "I'm a part-time conductor. I'm in the theater in St. Petersburg. At the moment I'm rehearsing *Boris Godunov*. But I'm not asleep."

"How come you're doing this job, then?"

"Because I have to make a living."

"As a conductor or an actor?"

The man shifted imperceptibly away from the window.

"I'm a conductor on the Paris–St. Petersburg run. The train stays in Russia for four days. For those four days, I'm an actor. I play the impostor in *Boris Godunov.*" He turned to Luca. "Looking for a woman?"

Luca didn't answer.

"When men seek me out in the middle of the night, it's usually because they want a woman."

Luca mumbled inaudibly. The conductor stared at him.

"I'm sorry," Luca said.

"No problem."

Luca turned away. The compartment seemed far away. Too far. He wished he could sink into it, losing himself in the twists and turns of his own journey.

He had never read *Boris Godunov.*

Luca closed his eyes and let his face go slack. Softly he whispered her name, again and again, like an unending rhyme—Anna, Anna, Anna. He remembered a poem by Osip Mandelstam that she'd read to him when they got back from London:

> *Your narrow shoulders will redden under scourges,*
> *Redden under scourges and burn in frosts.*
> *Your childlike arms will lift heavy irons,*
> *Lift heavy irons and sew mailbags.*

Your tender soles will walk barefoot on glass,
Barefoot on glass and blood-stained sand.

He murmured the verses to himself and remembered how she frowned as she recited, head bent, eyes closed. He listened as her voice faded into the mists of sinister omens, and imagined her coming close to him, rekindling their old desires. He could feel himself sliding his hand between her hair and her cheek, his index finger touching her earlobe, brushing the skin at that most intimate point.

He dozed on the seat, slumped against the paneling. Later, drifting in and out of a half sleep like soiled gauze, he stretched out on the berth, nestling his face in the crook of his arm.

For him sleep was a small death. He often put off going to bed as long as possible and, once ensconced between the sheets, he would deliberately seek to trigger his dreams, yearning to immerse himself in them as quickly and deeply as he could.

The only time he liked to sleep was when the emptiness of somnolence was the sole source of relief from the torments that assailed him. Then he dreaded waking, especially that inevitable instant just after the haze of reemergence lifted, when the entanglements you had tried to shake off coiled chokingly around you again.

Or when he slept beside a woman after draining himself of all energy with her and in her, and thought was drowned in the act. Love remedies evil presences. But there were few women beside whom he managed to fall asleep. Instead he would hold them close until, no longer able to forestall the moment of solitude, he would disengage himself from their arms and legs, from their skin and breath, and would turn to face a wall that brought back the dark of night, free of word or whisper.

Or when he killed time until the onset of oblivion by rummaging through ancient landscapes, trying to remember a little boy's toy cars, a garden in the countryside, his grandfather's Leica, the first great love of his life, and then the others, until the most recent, Valérie, with her disheveled auburn hair, sleeping there beside him on the mattress of their solitary dreams, her body touching his in an intimacy no longer shared.

Or when traveling on a train like this, half dozing, waiting for sleep to suppress all memory, for his youth to pass, until, exhausted, he could abandon himself to the cozy arc of his own arms, forming a semicircle like the train in Poznań station when the cart blocked his view of the face of a woman who may have been the ghost of Anna.

Or when increasingly shapeless, random images

sucked him into a whirling, rising spiral until all at once a door opens and he rises onto one elbow and asks, "What is it?"

"It's about the woman," a slightly shrill voice replied.

Luca sat up, trying to determine if he'd slept, and if so for how long.

"What woman are you looking for?"

"I'm not looking for any woman. Thanks anyway."

The actor-conductor stood in the doorway like a scarecrow, his arms braced against the frame.

"I was sleeping," Luca said apologetically.

"No problem. I was just thinking . . ."

The young man came into the compartment, slid the door closed behind him, and sat down on the opposite berth.

"Okay if I sit?" he asked. He stretched his legs out in front of him. "Mind if I smoke?"

He lit a cigarette. Beyond the windows, the hills were slowly turning white. The moon slipped in and out of clouds like frayed cloth. Luca wasn't sleepy anymore. He wondered whether she was still on the train, alone, sitting up or lying down, her head tilted back, with that slightly desperate sigh on her lips.

"I've seen all your films," the actor said. "Some I liked, others not."

Luca waved his hand. He didn't want to talk about that. The conductor waited. He took a slow drag on his cigarette.

"You must be pretty bored," Luca said.

"Well, you know. It's a thirty-five-hour trip."

They passed an enormous, gray-white cement factory lit by lamps and searchlights pointed upward. Wisps of smoke faded in the darkened sky. The buildings looked like prehistoric skeletons. Luca had noticed the same thing that first time, twenty years ago, when he was working on that first script.

He looked at the actor-conductor and said, "I'm planning on filming a Pushkin story, 'The Blizzard.' "

"I've read it. It's one of the *Tales of the Late Ivan Petrovich Belkin.*"

Luca was annoyed by the doubtful look in the young man's eyes. He himself had hesitated long enough. Countless times, at moments of great discouragement, he'd tried to convince himself that he had amassed too many ideas, too many bits and pieces of descriptions, lines of dialogue, and hypothetical sets to abandon a project so dear to him.

"The locations are all set," he said. "In St. Petersburg they gave me permission to shoot in a house Pushkin lived in back in 1831, near Pulkovo."

"In Tsarskoye Selo?"

"That's right."

It had taken three trips and five years of negotiation to get permission. He could have filmed the heroine's house anywhere, even in France, but he'd always wanted his *Blizzard* to be shot in St. Petersburg or its environs, near the city where Anna was born. Maybe it was his way of paying homage to her, partly because she had inspired the project, directly or indirectly, and partly to liberate himself by presenting such a painful story—endless, hopeless, and without sequel.

The young man watched a plume of cigarette smoke rise into the upper berths.

"So what about the girl?" he asked.

"There is no girl," Luca replied curtly.

"Tell me what she looks like."

He glanced at Luca, a touch of irony in his gaze.

"Long dark hair. Black dress, black shawl."

"That's not much to go on."

"It's all I know."

"Age?"

"Not sure."

"Height?"

"About five-six," he answered, almost without thinking.

"Like all women," the young man commented. "Name?"

"I don't know if she's married since . . ."

He gave it to him anyway.

"I'll give it some thought," the young man said, running his hand over his forehead. "It has to be this one?"

"None other," Luca said.

"It could be awhile. This train has a lot of passengers."

"It's possible she got off in Poznań."

"Then it'll take even longer."

Luca glanced surreptitiously at the young man, who carefully smoothed his pant legs.

Outside, the moon disappeared behind a cloud, making it glow from inside, a paler spot against a spindrift background. Luca smiled.

"I just remembered something else. She had a tiny white spot on her upper lip."

"This won't be easy."

"Like a drop of milk. A little star you can hardly see." He was silent for a moment. "She's very beautiful. Very touching."

"How long has it been since you've seen this woman?"

"A few hours ago. In the dining car."

"The spot might be gone." The young man uncrossed his arms, stood up, nodded vaguely, and repeated, "I'll give it some thought."

He left the compartment and walked silently down the corridor.

Luca closed the door and stretched out on the berth.

Or when, face down on a pillow as white as the ice of old memories, he saw a young girl's face, her smile, and the pink of her lips, with a very pale spot, like a pockmark in fine plaster.

Yes, she had that mark of rare delicacy on her upper lip. He noticed it one evening in the back room of the café, where he'd just finished a chess game. He told her there was a starburst on her lip. She laughed. "No, really," he insisted. "You have a spot on your lip."

"So what?" she asked, taking his hand.

"You don't give a damn that there's a spot on your lip?"

"Delible or indelible?"

He leaned close and kissed her, quickly licking her lips. Then he sat back and looked.

"Indelible."

She finished her coffee and stood up. He thought she was going to a mirror to examine her face, but she slipped on her coat and said, "Let's go."

In the street she took his arm.

"You'll have that spot all your life and you never even noticed!"

She stopped, turned to him, closed her eyes, and touched his face with her index finger.

"You have a little beauty mark here," she said. "And another one here. And a scratch just under the eyebrow, and a little spot behind your earlobe. Did you know that?"

She opened her eyes and took his arm again. They walked on. Luca wondered whether he could draw Anna's face with his eyes closed. He forgot the spot on her lip.

That night he took her to the club he sometimes went to in Saint-Michel. Until then he'd never felt like being there with her, possibly because it was his most secret spot, but possibly, too, because he knew she would feel out of place. But he wanted to show her that world.

When they came to a door pierced by a grilled

opening, she suddenly balked. "Where are we going?" she asked.

"To listen to some music," he said.

They walked into a swirl of noise, flashing lights, and people dancing. Luca led Anna to a table off to the side. She sat. He sat down across from her and put his hands on hers. She pulled them away. She looked at the dance floor with an impassive expression he'd never seen on her before.

Luca hailed a passing waiter and ordered a vodka on the rocks. He asked Anna what she wanted, but she didn't answer.

"Two vodkas," he told the waiter.

When the waiter left, Anna looked at Luca for the first time since they'd come in. "You go to places like this?" she asked.

"Sure," he replied, his voice even.

He realized he was treading a no man's land between war and peace. A few sideways steps—out the door and back into the street—would return them to the smooth terrain of their customary intimacy. But he didn't want to go. Anna sat transfixed, not far from the dancers, like an impeccably proper little girl lost among the electric rockers. He thought she looked ridiculous. He was right, she was wrong. He refused to apologize for an offense he hadn't committed.

"Often?"

"Yeah."

"And you like these places?"

"A lot."

She pushed her chair back a little.

"Have you been here since we met?"

"Once."

"To dance?"

"To listen to music."

"That's all?"

"What do you mean?"

"What is it you like about this place?"

He pointed to the dance floor and said, "That," pointed to the bar where a cluster of young people were laughing, and said, "That," pointed to the flashing lights that lit faces momentarily and dropped them back into darkness and said, "That," pointed to the waiter putting the two vodkas on the table and said, "Him."

He clinked his glass against Anna's.

"I don't want anything to drink. This is your world, not mine."

He downed his vodka in one gulp.

"Not my father, not my mother, none of us has ever been to a place like this."

She pointed at the dance floor. "We don't know how to dance."

She stared at him, anger rising in her gaze. "We sing," she went on. "We don't dance."

They stared at each other without a word. Then she made the gesture. Put her elbow on the table, rested her cheek in her palm, tilted her head back, and sighed deeply. Luca's defenses crumbled.

"This is ridiculous," he murmured.

He reached out his hand, but suddenly she stood up. They looked at each other, she standing, he still in his seat. Then she turned on her heels and headed for the exit. He didn't move.

He drank Anna's vodka, then ordered another, and another. He pictured her in the street, trying to find her way on the map at the Saint-Michel métro station, then alone in a second-class car, and at the Saint-Lazare station. He wondered whether it had all ended here, in a little corner of his home turf.

He joined the dancers on the floor. The spotlights were like flashes of lightning revealing Anna's face. He shrugged.

Later, in the dark and empty Sunday night streets, he thought about her, about her body and the way it felt against his. Like this, he said to her in his mind's eye: my hand on the nape of your neck, tight like a fist, your face on my shoulder, your arm on my back, my other hand caressing your hips, lulling you to sleep.

That was his image of her.

On the train back to the suburbs he huddled into a shell where he thought she couldn't reach him. It's over, he said to himself, over. But other desires soon came upon him. He hoped he'd find her standing there on the platform, or on the way to The Garden, or asleep in the hollow of his mattress.

But he didn't.

Indelible, Luca thought as he dropped onto the bed.

When he awoke his hand roamed the mattress, seeking her in vain. Her body was missing.

At five o'clock that afternoon he went out. A nasty wind rustled the trees. He walked along streets, avenues, and sidewalks, passing not far from where she lived, wandering through the mid-level managers' housing development. He stopped at a café, had a tea at the counter, and tried to think of some reason to ring her bell. He could say he wanted to borrow a book, the Solex, anything.

It started to rain. His hair was streaming when he entered the back room of the café. He sat down near the windows, where the players were, and pretended to study a board from which the pieces had not been taken, three moves from mate: queen to d8, pawn to b6, bishop to cover the rook.

She came in at seven. He almost waved to her,

but she barely glanced at him before sitting down at a distant table. She took out her notebook and began to draw. Her face was incredibly impassive. She was very pale. Luca thought her hand trembled a bit as she drew. For some reason he couldn't fathom, he vaguely sensed something else, something not related simply to their story. He watched her surreptitiously, hoping that when she finished her drawing she would get up and join him. Minutes passed. She pulled out a new sheet of paper but did not get up. It was as though he didn't exist. She leaned over, opened her purse, and put her notebook away. He waited, sure that now she would come. He pushed the chessboard to the edge of the table to make room for her. But she stood, slung her purse over her shoulder, and disappeared through the door to the front room without so much as a glance at him.

Luca still didn't move. His legs were lead, his stomach hurt. All his energy, as fierce as it was ephemeral, melted in the hollow of his chest like a sugar cube in warm water.

He looked up. A man stood beside the table. Luca recognized the silver hair, the breast-pocket handkerchief, and the blue eyes, as immobile and frigid as a soulless ice floe. It was the man he'd played the evening he met Anna.

"Care for a game?"

The man put his hands on the table and waited. In a flash Luca thought to himself: If I win, I win Anna. If I lose, I lose Anna.

"Okay," he said.

In his own mind he amended the stakes: If I win, I win Anna, but I never play again; if I lose, I lose Anna, but I keep playing.

The man sat down. He picked up a black pawn and a white pawn, hid them behind his back, and said, "Which hand?"

"The left," Luca replied.

The fingers of his left hand wandered gently over the seat cover. He felt a very old sensation, like being wrapped in a soothing black and white veil of soft cotton. It was as though he were back in the café, as in the old days, and just as in the old days, he could seal himself off from all distractions, forgetting the smoking stove in the middle of a room, the jukebox playing Cat Stevens or Bob Dylan, and even Anna, forgetting what it was he was about to lose and abandoning himself to a pure joy he hadn't felt for twenty years, a joy his left hand now rediscovered on the train seat early that morning as Paris drew near.

Luca looked at his fingers, smiled fleetingly, and whispered to himself: e2-e4, e7-e5, g1-f3, b8-c6. His left hand moved as though over a chessboard, mimicking ancient gestures. Luca let it move, utterly rapt by the magic he had deliberately denied himself, thereby mutilating himself forever after playing the final but most beautiful game of his life.

$\sim$

*H*e picked black. His partner seemed truly sorry. A few other players came over and stood around the table. They knew Luca. His opponent was not one of them.

White moved his king's pawn two squares forward. Everyone expected an Italian or French defense, a king's gambit, or some other classical opening. Luca had other plans. He moved his knight to f6, launching a variation of the King's Indian defense. A murmur swept through the room. White glanced at his opponent, shrugged in annoyance, and moved his queen's pawn one square forward, protecting himself while bolstering his position in the center. The onlookers now expected Luca to reply with a variation of the

Alekhine defense. They were taken aback when he moved his queen's bishop's pawn to c5.

Anna. Anna that day at the pond.

They all looked at one another. Newcomers joined the circle around the table.

White consolidated his hold on the center by advancing another pawn. He stared at Luca with a glint of irony.

Luca put his hands flat on the table. He ceded control of the center and began playing at the edges, distributing his pieces awkwardly. Just like at the beginning, when she called him *vous* and they were struggling to discover each other. Before the Solex.

White castled on the seventh move. Luca followed suit. The black king was protected by a knight, a bishop, a rook, and three pawns forming a triangle. It was a solid defense, unassailable if he made no mistake. It would be a long game. The story of their love should have been as long.

White offered a pawn exchange that Black declined, preferring to move his king onto the bishop's diagonal. There was plenty of time. You don't lose the love of your life one-two-three. If it had to end here, let it at least be a beautiful game! Let it be memorable!

He looked at White.

White studied the board for a very long time,

then took a black pawn. Black took back immediately, though with his queen, not the knight, as White expected. "I was born in Leningrad." The accent. His grandfather's accent. Her look, her hair, her hand on his neck. The spot on her lip. A starburst.

White touched his watchband. He glanced briefly at the spectators and then at Luca, who watched the board impassively. Four pieces were in play: two knights, a bishop, a queen. White marshaled his pieces to support the developing knot. So did Black. They maneuvered for control of the center-left of the board, but with no direct confrontation, as if preparing for a later offensive. "Tomorrow we'll tell each other different things."

On the tenth move White withdrew his queen. Black withdrew his, and both knights retreated. The knot unraveled, the onlookers sighed, a floorboard creaked. Luca didn't budge. Anna came into the room. Luca raised his left hand. It hung there, suspended, for a few seconds, then fell upon a knight and moved it forward. He put his hand on the table and waited. "I'm glad it's only temporary."

White was surprised. He calculated possibilities, let a minute pass, then two, then three. Finally he took a pawn at d4, and before he knew it Luca's left hand was in motion again, occupying square d5.

That morning, at the green door, when they fell

into each other's arms and he whispered, "I'm crazy about you," and she answered, "I'm crazy about you."

Anna stood there, not far away, not moving. By now everyone in the café had gathered around the table. She watched too. The others would have said that Black was playing quickly and accurately. They might have described his gestures, evaluated his degree of concentration, but no more than that. Anna, however, saw everything. Luca's eyelid fluttered imperceptibly, as though gauging a threat. He was solemn and unbearably tense. She knew he was racked by an inner torment, an unyielding turmoil of the spirit.

He stared unblinking at the board. Black launched a thrust with his queen. White retreated; Black took a piece; White took back. Black blocked the file of the queen's rook. White settled somewhat in his seat, and that was when Luca and Anna glanced at each other for an instant above the assembled faces and silhouettes. But she made no sign to him, and he turned back to the game. She had never seen that glint in his eyes before, expressing a force, a mad desire, wholly alien to him.

She edged closer. No one paid any attention to her. White attacked Black's center pawn, accepted the exchange offered by his opponent, lost a pawn and took one back.

When he felt her cheek, from jaw to chin, palm

flat against her skin. When she touched his neck with her index finger, when she put their hands together and said, "We love each other," when he kissed her mouth and the side of her nose, her cheekbone and her eyelid, when she talked about her parents, when he looked for a present to buy her, when she teased him until anger lines appeared on his brow.

Right hand, left hand. Little by little Black occupied all the board's strategic points. White responded to each move with equivalent shifts and repositionings of his own pieces.

She said, "I love white tulips, that you hold my hand, and spring and fall, I love white chocolate, I don't like it when you're sad or when you think about chess when you talk to me, I don't like mountains and greenery, I like rivers and cities better, I don't like it when you pretend not to love me anymore, I like desire, I don't like plans, I love you, yes, I love you."

Bewildered, White fine-tuned his defense. Left hand: Black stationed his knight midway between his king and one of his rooks. The remaining enemy bishop was pinned to f3. White set out to queen one of his pawns. On the sixty-seventh move Luca blocked the way. On the seventieth he began exchanging pieces. Murmurs swept through the room. Black exchanged a bishop for a rook, a rook for a rook. Then, to general disbelief, he tilted his chair back and gave a little snort perceptible to the two front ranks of on-lookers. Anna heard it, froze, pondered it. But he didn't look at her. He didn't need to. He was playing for her and her alone, offering her the rooks, knights, bishops, kings, and queens of his childhood.

Very few pieces remained on the board. Luca now moved as quickly as if he were playing rapid transit. On the seventy-ninth move White's king was trapped on b2, and he lost a pawn. Having now recovered his impassive mask, Luca lifted his right hand, pushed a pawn from c5 to c4, put his hands flat on the table, and smiled.

His opponent stared glumly at the position, frowned, and tipped over his king in resignation.

The regulars burst into applause. Luca stood up. He glanced at the board, turned to find Anna, took her by the hand, and led her out.

In the street he looked at her and whispered, "I'm taking you to London. Call it a honeymoon. From now on we'll never be apart."

She didn't move. All she said was, "Yes, take me. Take me forever."

That night she gave him the first and only gift he ever got from her: a Russian edition of Pushkin's short stories. Three days later, on the ferry across the Channel, she read "The Blizzard" to him.

two

He got off in Brussels, the last stop before Paris. The big clock in the station said four in the morning. He went to the snack bar, eager to escape the long ribbon of the train, the clock, the shadowy dance of travelers drifting back and forth alongside the cars. He had an image of Anna joining him in another station, in London, under another clock with black numbers, one he remembered as even bigger than this one.

He saw a hand on the counter a few inches from his own.

"How come you didn't fly? It's such a long trip by train . . ."

He replied that long ago, when he first started traveling, he used to yearn for the moment when the plane unleashed its power on the runway and hurtled into the sky as the cars of his adolescence hurtled down empty highways. But eventually he tired of it. He didn't like flying anymore.

"It would have been easier on a plane. Not as many people.

"Do you go to Leningrad often?" he asked when he saw Luca wasn't going to say anything.

Luca said he did. The name had been changed, but he was happy to hear those three syllables again: Le-nin-grad.

"Somewhere Brodsky talks about two statues opposite one another, one in the Finland Station, the other in Bierovich Park. The first is Peter the Great astride a horse, the second Lenin perched on a tank."

"In the sixteenth century wars were fought on horseback," Luca replied. "Different eras, that's all."

The actor-conductor looked at him with a kindly frown. "Let me buy you a coffee."

Luca ordered two.

"There are several hundred passengers on this train, most of them still asleep. That makes it hard to spot a white mark on a lip."

"I didn't ask you to," Luca snapped.

They drank their coffee.

"Why are you doing this?"

"It breaks up the trip. And it's a change from the usual gentlemen who want a lady for a night. I'm not a procurer."

The actor-conductor put down his cup, broke a sugar cube in half, put one piece in his mouth, and turned to Luca.

"I'm not going to ask you why you're looking for this woman, but I would like to know if you're *really* looking for her."

Luca didn't say a word.

"Because if you want to find someone on a train, I can tell you how to do it. It's not that difficult."

"I'm looking for her because I want to offer her a part."

"The role of her life?"

"No, of mine."

Luca tried to pay, but the young man stopped him. He put some coins on the counter.

"Leave me your address and remind me what her name was," he said. "I'll check it out at the office."

Luca scribbled the information on a page of his notebook, and they went back to the platform. The actor smiled, raised his hand in a half salute, and disappeared into one of the cars.

Luca walked to the front of the train, trying to peer through the windows, some of which were shielded by blinds. He saw unlikely silhouettes, male or female he couldn't tell. He got on and headed down the corridors as the train shook itself into motion. He walked slowly, staring now at the carpet, now at the darkened windows of the compartments. He began to move a little faster, brushing a door handle, a window-pane. Then he stopped, lingering in the vestibule between cars, loosening the knot of his scarf and letting himself be jostled by the rocking and the curves. He realized he hadn't shaved or washed, had barely eaten or slept, and had done no work since leaving St. Petersburg two evenings ago. He had thought of her without respite, relentlessly. Suddenly it seemed intolerable to be so near a kind of closure without bringing this story to its natural conclusion. He went into the next car, stepped onto the carpet, opened the door of the first compartment, and leaned in. He looked, excused himself, closed the door, and opened the next one, continuing through that car and into the next, on and on, looking in on reclining shapes, surprising sleepy faces, watching bodies disappear under blankets, interrupting people getting dressed and others sitting erect.

The train was passing through less and less depopulated areas. There were a few hamlets, then a village, then another. Luca continued his quest as daylight dawned, desperate because Paris was drawing near, and when empty landscapes gave way to Apollinaire, long orphanage of stations, she would be lost to him a second time.

And the long orphanage of stations approached, the gloomy suburbs where Luca had spent his gloomy childhood years. Baggage was being piled in the corridors, and he hadn't found her, hadn't had any luck at all.

He went back to his compartment, got his suitcase, and went out into the corridor, jostling other passengers and clearing himself a path. He was the first one off the train.

He stood at the front end of the platform alongside the sighing locomotive and peered at the crowd streaming past. He stayed until the last passenger had gone.

Then he wandered through the station for a long moment until finally, at seven o'clock, he went to the taxi stand, got into a cab, and said, "Rue Campagne-Première, just before the Lion de Belfort."

He went home.

As he looked out at the city, his old habits returned. It was like going into a house he knew belonged to him. At first the rooms felt chilly, but as they neared the Seine, he savored the sense of reassurance that always came when he entered familiar territory—a touch of dread at the dark mass of the Conciergerie, up Saint-Michel, then the Luxembourg Gardens with their gates of gilded pikes, Montparnasse and Vavin, left at the Boulevard Raspail, along the tree-bordered service road, and another hundred yards to Rue Campagne-Première.

He paid the driver, got out, and walked along the street.

Usually he enjoyed coming home, but when he opened the door that day, his pleasure was tinged with a fleeting distaste.

A couple of friends were asleep on the convertible bed in the living room. They lived in Bordeaux and had told him they were coming. They lay next to each other, eyes closed, her body diagonal on the mattress. She had one hand on her husband's face, index and middle fingers against his cheek.

He was touched by their loving abandon. He never would have suspected it of them, and perhaps he envied it. He walked through the tidy kitchen and down the hallway to his room. He started to go in, barely glimpsed Valérie's sleeping shape, and backed out, quickly closing the door.

He went into the bathroom. He wanted to be alone, to enjoy not so much the momentary solitude now left to him, but the deeper loneliness of which he would soon be deprived. He wished there were nothing and no one to rob him of his time, wished he could do or not do whatever he pleased—dream, read the papers, look at the Montparnasse tower from the attic window, wander naked through the rooms, sleep, squander the dose of freedom that should have been his.

He undressed and ran a bath, remembering that a woman once pointed out that he never folded his clothes and recalling that his girlfriends always tried to make him dress the way they wanted, urging him to abandon his old brands for new ones to which he happily sacrificed his earlier preferences, delighted to be dressed and undressed like the dolls they no longer played with.

The warm water was an ineffable pleasure. He lay in the tub, his body submerged, eyes closed, face impassive. He thought of the faces of the women he had loved enough to be with the day after, when he would lie like this, the back of his neck against the tiles, and watch them put on their makeup at the mirror over the sink. The misted glass always seemed to engulf them in a haze that melded gestures, words, and expressions. But some things stood out. The way one of them, a tall, thin brunette, delicately pursed her lips to apply a crimson lipstick which she touched up with a fine brush, and the way another patted her cheeks with a puff of soft pink rice powder, which she then put back into a case before drawing thin black lines at the corners of her eyelids. The first was Anna, the second his mother.

*H*e got out of the bath and was about to grab a towel when he heard a door close. Valérie's footsteps got louder as they came down the hallway. He climbed back into the tub, stretched out again, let his head sink under the water, and held his breath. When he reemerged he heard knocking.

"Luca? Is that you? Luca?"

He didn't answer. Then he said no, it wasn't him.

Her big leather purse lay on the kitchen table. Luca looked at it with some distress. She'd had it with her the first time he saw her. She'd been wearing a long dress and leather boots, leaning against a pillar in the apartment of a mutual acquaintance who'd invited them and others to dinner. She had a clear gaze, short auburn hair, and a charming, childlike way of raising the cigarette he offered her to the middle of her lips, inhaling diligently, eyes closed. She had the touching beauty of a woman nearing forty, with that special solemnity that lay over her features like a tint, a tiny vulnerability.

They'd had the requisite dinner—appetizer, main course, cheese, dessert—after which their host suggested liqueur and they talked in fits and starts of the world and its problems.

He looked at her and was touched by the purse, the dress, and the boots, which reminded him of the ones women wore in the seventies.

After a while he went over to her and said, "I know you're not comfortable here; otherwise you wouldn't be smoking. You're not a smoker. Why don't we get out of here?"

They left. She laughed in the elevator and in the street. "It had to be salmon," she said. "In that kind of dinner they always serve salmon."

He followed the usual script, and she accepted. They both knew why they were taking the same taxi to the same address—his—and they both knew what they would do without a word when they got there, after which they would talk about something else, and when she left he would think about her.

He pondered it with a feeling he mistook for tenderness. She undressed by herself, slipped between the sheets, and looked at him, waiting. They screwed for a long time, without the usual first-time modesty, without poetry or embarrassment, despite a somewhat dignified reserve that grew as time passed and they did it again and again. There was a slightly forced natural-ness about it, less pure desire than a need to affirm a kind of licentiousness with gestures immediately coun-tered by tiny withdrawals: a shielding elbow, an ill-placed hand, a painful mouth. He found it took some effort to throw himself into what soon came to seem like a demonstration, desire accompanied by fear.

But it was not tenderness he felt; it was pity.

⁓

*V*alérie joined him in the kitchen, closing the door behind her so as not to wake the others. She came over and hugged him, and after an imperceptible hesitation, he put his arms around her. In several months they'd gone beyond the emotional demonstra-tiveness of the early days but had not yet reached the perfunctory pecks Luca found so horrifying. They were not living together—an arrangement she saw as a way of rationing their relationship. He saw it as a way of rationing their time of love.

Assuming they loved each other.

He made coffee. She tightened the belt of her

robe and sat down. Actually it was his robe. At first he was touched when she wore it. Now it left him indifferent. He dreaded the moment when indifference would become exasperation.

She asked about his trip and he answered as best he could, talking about places instead of people. He told her about the train, the conductor, St. Petersburg in winter. "What about your film?" she interrupted. "Are you going to make it?"

"Of course."

He never liked talking about his scripts, whether before, during, or after. In advance he found it almost impossible to summarize the plot, structure, and characters, not to mention all the technical problems that would come up and the changes that would be made as the work progressed. During the shooting he was so absorbed in these complexities that no one could grasp the degree of his uncertainty. Once the film was made, he had nothing to add.

He felt trapped, so he got up, suggested toast and orange juice, then sat back down and looked at her. She smiled at him. For a long time he had found that smile winning; even now his defenses crumbled as he looked into her eyes. Suddenly he felt better.

"I almost forgot!" he exclaimed. "I brought you something."

She put a finger to her lips and whispered, "You'll wake your friends."

They laughed. Luca stood up, went behind Valérie, raised her by her shoulders, turned her around, and took her in his arms.

He suggested to his friends that they all go to Saint-Germain-en-Laye for lunch. He knew it sounded strange—the forest in winter—but he managed to convince them without too much swordplay.

They drove in silence, taking the beltway around Paris, past La Défense, and out Route 13. Luca stared out at the roads, which he had traveled on foot, on the Solex, and in other people's cars long before he acquired one of his own. The avenues were sad and gloomy, the trees wept their winter tears. He felt no nostalgia, only a mute depression fueled by images long dead. He didn't like the scenery of his youth.

They turned off at Saint-Germain-en-Laye, followed the road past the residence for mid-level managers and the other building, where her uncle and aunt lived. The premises seemed smaller now, almost cramped. But he felt a tug at his heart when he saw the gate, the stairs, and the third window from the right on the fifth floor.

He closed his eyes.

When they got to the foot of the slope, he told the driver to turn left. They went through a bypass that wasn't there before, and he pointed to a small cream-colored building. As the car slowed, it occurred to him that some stories cannot be shared, that his friends would feel nothing except perhaps a vague curiosity about someone else's memories. He was sorry he hadn't come alone.

When he first went in, he recognized nothing. The counter had changed, the staff was different, and the place seemed charmless. But then he took a closer look, admitting to himself that it was probably equally charmless then. As always in these idiotic comparisons, you remember the places of the past as larger than they really were, and they seem shrunken when you see them again, commensurate with your own disappointed expectations.

But then he heard a faint sound unlike any other, and a smile lit his face.

"This way," he said, leading his friends into the back room. He stood at the threshold and studied the scene as though it were a set in a film he was writing. The tables were the same, laid out in exactly the same way as before. The jukebox was gone, and the stove had been replaced by an electric radiator, but players still raised and lowered their hands over the clocks that timed their moves. Luca was suddenly paralyzed with emotion. He stood there for a long moment, motionless, prey to a strange happiness.

Then he turned to Valérie, put his hand on her shoulder, and said, "This was a bad idea. Let's go home."

Back in Paris he offered clumsy excuses and left his friends without worrying about what they would do or whether he would see them again. He needed to be alone.

At home he locked himself in his office and re-read the notes he'd made in that spiral notebook twenty years ago. He now added others, shaping the structure of the first half of the script, from their encounter at a Young Pioneers meeting in a Leningrad café to their departure for Kishinev, Bessarabia, which would stand in for London.

He could visualize the café: two rooms, customers in one, chess players in the other, a fireplace, no music, narrow windows, roughcast walls, a chilly atmosphere symbolically warmed by the girl's entrance. She wears an astrakhan coat trimmed with cheap fur, and a thick, soft turtleneck. No kilt. No mohair sweater.

The young man is already at the Young Pioneers meeting when she comes in—late. But Luca put him aside for the moment.

Next Tsarskoye Selo, where he would shoot. The young man's home: half a room in a communal lodging. He wouldn't be a soldier, but a composer. An orphan. Later he would vanish into the Siberian tundra (or elsewhere). The Solex would be replaced by a bicycle (if need be). He would keep the chess, less as dramatic support than as the perceptible evidence of change.

During the early months of their love, they take walks: the corridors of the Hermitage, Ostrovsky Square, from bridge to bridge, from the Russian Museum to the Smolny Institute, from the Admiralty to Arts Square, through the Field of Mars, the gardens of the Bronze Horseman, the Manezh, Basil's Island.

And so on.

Then they leave. Probably for reasons related to the young man's chess playing. Not for London, but Kishinev, the city to which Pushkin was exiled from 1820 to 1823. The city where Luca's grandfather was born.

The rest was harder to figure out. Not that it was indefinite or uncertain, but he wasn't sure of the form. As he'd thought about it over the years, Luca could never decide whether to use an off-screen voice, a flashback, alternating scenes in real time, free invention, or whether, on the contrary, he should stick closely to the reality he knew so well, having learned of it in a letter from Anna's mother in a hotel room in Piccadilly in 1971.

Luca went to the foyer, took a ring of keys from a nail, and rode the elevator to the basement. He looked for the door to the storage room, found it on the third try, and made his way into a fetid concrete stall shielded from humidity. Here he kept old files, alternative versions of his screenplays, a few reels, and a secret or two.

Atop a shelf was an iron box. Luca took it. He also took a projector and an old screen whose existence he had forgotten. He took them back to his apartment and opened the iron box. Inside were things that belonged to Anna: a black velvet headband, a pencil with a tiny Russian doll on the eraser end, an embroidered white handkerchief with an ink stain, a false sapphire, a glass earring, two letters, and three reels of Super-8 film.

Luca set the screen up against the bookshelf, finding no joy in ancient gestures that seemed as out-dated as his first material. He unfolded the tripod, pressed the button, raised the pole, unrolled the beaded screen, and hooked it into place. Then he put the projector on the desk, turned it to face the screen, and removed the cover. It took a long time to position the beam of light properly, and more than one attempt to thread the reel. Then he drew the blinds, doused the lights, and turned on the machine. Images flickered on the screen, finally stabilizing to reveal the three-quarter profile of a girl leaning against the railing of a ship.

Anna, April 1971, on the day they left for England.

Luca had bought his first movie camera the night before. A Paillard Bolex Super-8. He'd tried it out in his room in The Garden but lost the test film during one of his many moves. All that remained were three silent reels.

The first was taken on the ferry and the train, the other two in London.

Anna is looking at the sea. She wears a scarf, a light, cream-colored linen dress, flat loafers. She sports a somewhat solemn smile.

She turns to Luca and hides her face, apparently asking him to stop shooting. But he doesn't. She runs laughing along the railing, stumbles, rights herself. The image is unsteady as Luca follows her to the end of the deck. Then it goes black. They were probably kissing.

Anna sitting on a chair, scribbling one of her countless drawings. Zoom in on the face, long pause, and her left hand moves quickly over the paper to hide what she's drawing; zoom back, head shot: Anna concentrating, her face betraying a kind of severity; she's forgotten she's being filmed. Her hair is tied into a bun. Now she's wearing a navy-blue coat, the collar turned up against the wind. She shivers, raises her head, sees Luca, and smiles.

Anna reading a story, translating it from the Russian for Luca. Pushkin's "The Blizzard." Closeup of the face, then the lips. The tiny, touching white spot is visible.

Anna waiting in line to get off the ferry.

Anna handing her ticket to an off-screen ticket taker.

Anna carrying two suitcases, her own and Luca's. She puts them down and turns to him. He seems to be a long way off. She puts her fists on her hips, leans forward, and stares at him with a frown tinged with mockery, tenderness, and exasperation.

Luca, from the rear, a suitcase in either hand.

Anna on the train, sleeping, cheek on her shoulder, hair hiding her face. Her lips are slightly parted, as though tracing the shadow of a smile.

Anna, still on the train. The camera is on the other side of the glass of the compartment; Luca is shooting from the corridor. Anna's pad of paper rests on her knees. She is drawing. Suddenly she puts her pencil down, brings her hand to the nape of her neck, presses her fingers against the skin, tilts her head back, closes her eyes.

Anna looking at Luca, her face propped in her hands. She stares at him without blinking. It was a game they used to play: who would blink first. Her eyes are wider and wider. They get moist, then wet. Tears sprout on the lashes. She quits when they run down her cheeks. Then she grimaces and mouths three words, separating the syllables so Luca can easily understand: I-love-you.

Anna on the platform at Victoria Station. Luca is hiding behind a pillar. She is looking for him. The suitcases are at her feet. She stands beneath a huge clock with black numerals. He zooms in and catches her face, full frame. In her expression he sees disarray, then fear and the front edge of panic. She sees him and makes a funny face, sullen and charming.

Anna in the first flat they rented in London, a small room in a house owned by a landlady who reminded Luca of the widow at The Garden. She would take only singles, and Luca pretended to be alone. The first night he helped Anna climb over the balustrade. The second night they got caught.

Anna astride the balustrade, shot from outside. She is about to leap into the room when the door opens. The landlady appears, waving her arms. You can tell she is screaming. Anna hesitates and then drops back to the street. Luca is still filming. The landlady goes to the window, raises her arms to the sky, beckons to a passing witness. Anna laughs. Her face beams with intense happiness, joy, enchantment. The girl is doubled over in hysterical laughter as the old Englishwoman slams the shutters. The camera keeps rolling. Luca could see from the unstable image that he was laughing too.

Blackout.

Anna crossing an avenue in London. Luca shoots from inside a taxi. You can see the driver's shoulder. Anna goes into a hotel.

Cut.

Anna coming out of the hotel. With her finger she signals, No.

Anna going into another hotel, then coming out to the taxi, shaking her head.

Anna going into a third hotel. She shrugs.

A street in Piccadilly. High angle shot. The camera pans and returns to the interior of a room. Anna comes out of the shower, naked. When she sees Luca, she hurriedly covers herself, right hand over her crotch, left arm across her breasts.

Blackout.

Anna, in panties, at the bathroom mirror, delicately pursing her lips to apply a crimson lipstick, putting the final touches on with a fine brush. She taps her cheeks to give herself some color, picks up a brush, leans forward, and disentangles her long dark locks.

Anna on the upper level of a double-decker bus.

Anna in Regents Park.

Anna eating a muffin at an outdoor café. Closeup. She turns to the camera and speaks. Luca remembered the words: "I'm eighteen, I'm from Leningrad, I live in Paris, I'm now in London, I'm in love with a nut, I have three dresses, four blouses, a coat, no money, and no fear."

Anna and Luca at a mirror, probably in their hotel room. He is teaching her how to use the camera.

He has on baggy jeans and a dark crew-neck sweater. His hair is long. He looks very tall standing beside her. She comes up to his shoulder. She brings her mouth close to his and they kiss as he shoots into the mirror. She kisses him on the temple. He hands the camera, still running, to Anna. She takes it, peers through the viewfinder. He takes two steps backward. She turns to him.

Luca, full frame. He puts his hands on either side of his face, thumbs along his cheeks. He comes nearer. The image moves. Anna turns back to the mirror. Shot of the ceiling.

Blackout.

Wide-angle shot of the hotel room. They've probably been there a few days. A succession of images:

Anna turning her back to slip on a nightgown that comes to mid-thigh.

Luca in bed. He wakes up, turns his head right and left, opens his eyes, smiles at the camera. Then he gets out of bed, naked.

Anna asleep, lying on her back, her hand groping the mattress in search of a body that isn't there.

Anna straightening the bedspread with a brief sweep of the flat of her hand.

Luca slumped in an armchair, legs draped over the armrests.

Luca in the doorway.

Anna casting a glance around the room before leaving.

Anna checking that the cap on the tube of toothpaste is on tight.

Anna leaning close to the bathroom mirror, putting on eyeshadow.

Luca pondering a chessboard.

Anna choosing a pair of tights.

Anna carefully folding her things at night.

They're laughing. Luca remembered why: they were playing grownups, mimicking gestures they'd seen their parents make. When Anna played, Luca could tell she was acting, because her face would take on an expression he'd never seen before, a very slight stiffening of the features, a fleeting authority that faded almost immediately. But it was an expression he hadn't been able to capture. They didn't stay long enough in London.

*L*ast reel.

Piccadilly. Anna in the street. An overcast sky. She's wearing her navy-blue coat and a black sweater he'd bought for her the day before. She raises her head and looks for Luca, who is shooting from the hotel room. She waves at him several times, her hand moving in a wide arc above her head. Then she disappears, on her way to the post office to pick up the mail she's had forwarded from Paris.

Same point of view. The camera frames a silhouette in the street, picking it out among others. Zoom in. It's Anna. You can see by her coat. She's walking very fast. Her face is invisible. She jostles a passerby, turns into the hotel, disappears.

The door of the room, full frame. It flies open. Anna stands there, crying, her face ravaged. She is motionless, as though paralyzed. In her fist she holds a few sheets of paper and a newspaper clipping.

Blackout.

Luca let the last reel spin when it ended. It took him an eternity to get up from the desk, go to the window, open the blinds, and turn off the machine. He had to make an even greater effort not to rethread the film, close the blinds, and begin again.

He went to the attic. The Montparnasse tower loomed not far away, luminous in the gathering dusk. Luca picked up his spiral notebook, slipped on a coat, and went out. He wanted to be alone, without Valérie and without his friends.

He walked down the Boulevard Montparnasse, went into the Sélect, picked a table in the back room, and sat down. He took out his notebook and jotted a few things down. If he had to shoot it, he'd do it this way:

Anna at the threshold of the London hotel room on that last day. She's crying. Her face is ravaged. She is motionless, as though paralyzed. In her fist she holds a few sheets of paper and a newspaper clipping.

Luca goes to her, pulls her into the room. She says nothing. He asks no questions. He holds her. She cries on his shoulder. Suddenly she pulls away.

She puts the sheets of paper down on the table and sinks to the floor near the bed, knees pulled up to her chin, her head turning slowly from left to right. She has stopped crying, but murmurs, "No, no, no," like a scansion, a stifled shout.

Luca looks at the newspaper clipping. He sees a man's photo and a headline in Cyrillic letters. He reads the last page of her mother's letter.

> *On the trolley ride home from that wretched airport that we've never gone back to since, your father said we would never see you again. When parents put children into this world, he said, they know it's only a matter of time until they break away. With us it*

happened early, since our little girl left at eighteen. But we had chosen your destiny ourselves.

For days and days and even longer, your father couldn't bear seeing things that belonged to you. He put away your books, hid your dolls under the bed, took your photographs down from the bookshelves. He said he couldn't live in a place where everything reminded him of you. Then there were other days, for an even longer time, when he felt it was impossible to live in a house without a hint of your presence. So he put everything back. That's how it was: from one kind of pain to another, from surfeit to lack, he tried to survive without you. He couldn't mention his daughter without his voice breaking. He said that your leaving was a disaster, a lifelong mourning. It was like having a limb amputated: he would try to touch a familiar part of his body and would find it gone, an elusive shadow, like caressing a void.

When sorrow choked him he would go to the river and call your name. One night some policemen stopped him. He cursed them, and they beat him up. That's how it all began. That night your father slept in what used to be your room, in what used to be your bed. He said he used to be your father, that you used to be his daughter, and that he would never see you again.

The next day they searched the place and found the manuscript he'd been working on since you left: "Nights of the World," an homage to this century, "my century, my brute," as Mandelstam put it. Three days later they came to get us.

You can read the story of the trial in the clipping. I'm leaving today with your father. Write to us.

Luca kneels down next to Anna and tries to hold her. She pushes him away. He falls back. She comes to him and puts her arms around his shoulders. She says her father has been sentenced to ten years' hard labor, that he's been found guilty of parasitism and anti-Soviet propaganda. She says she wants Luca to copy her mother's letter so he can make a film of it some-day. She says her parents need her, that she can't leave them alone. There is a kind of pride in her voice, as though she is preparing for a very long battle. She says she's going home. She says: "They've cut off my legs."

They went back to Paris. They spent the last night in his room at The Garden. They didn't eat or sleep. They lay on the bed, dressed, and held each other. They didn't speak. They waited for daybreak with dread.

When it came time, Luca went with Anna to the airport.

She wore the black turtleneck from that first day. They didn't look into each other's eyes. They separated without a word, without a gesture, in an airport corridor. He stood there paralyzed as she walked away.

Suddenly she turned, put her suitcase down, and came slowly back to him. They held each other with desperate strength. When she was in his arms, her mouth in the hollow of his neck, he felt warm tears on his skin and thought she was about to change her mind, but she took his face in her hands, held it so he could come no closer, and said in a voice nearly inaudible, with pain in her eyes, her teeth chattering, "I'll never forget you."

Then she walked away, very slowly.

As he left the airport he thought to himself, I am a layered mountain of burials, one stratum of sorrow, another of life, another of sorrow.

And suddenly it all shifted like quicksand.

He walked along the road that skirted the runways, feeling as though he now had to add an even more terrible layer to the shit already accumulated. Or else everything would collapse. Everything meaning himself.

He went back to their suburb, got the Solex, drove it into the underground parking garage of the residence for mid-level managers, picked the straightest ramp, disengaged the motor, and pedaled silently and as fast as he could toward a concrete wall. As he picked up speed, he opened his eyes wide, straining to see it all, to miss nothing. Gasping for breath, saying, "Anna, Anna, Anna, for always, for always," he split his forehead open on a gray wall.

Luca closed his notebook and left the Sélect. It was pouring rain. He now knew how to structure the second half of his film. He also knew what game he'd play with his audience, keeping them at a slight distance from the real heart of the story, telling it in fits and starts. He would present events that hadn't happened as though they had, shift them imperceptibly forward in the narrative, thus creating deceitful doubts. Sometimes he would seem to wander off on tangents, slipping into digressions on apparently secondary facts that were actually as essential as grace notes sometimes are. He would muddy certain tracks that would be clarified three scenes or twenty pages later, thus leading those who followed him to draw up alongside him and move slightly ahead of him. He would even help them sniff out that strange something that they now knew defined the story they were discovering. Finally, having duly warned them, he would close the cover of his Russian dolls and take them somewhere else—past the Vavin intersection, for example, and left on the Boulevard Raspail, to a calm and tranquil place where appearances had not yet assumed the expected form.

Valérie was sitting on the sofa in the studio, wearing a light T-shirt, her feet pulled up against her. He sat down in an armchair opposite her and suddenly realized that tonight he didn't love her. He could tell by the bangs that fell over her forehead and by her complexion, tinged with gray in the room's shadows. He was angry with himself for reacting to trivialities that, as he well knew, concealed far more.

A storm grumbled outside. "I'm going home," Valérie said.

But she didn't move.

An intense despair overtook Luca at the notion that he was once again about to reenact the breakup scenario. It would be no fun, he knew, and he wished it could be different, wished he could change, that the women around him, the ones in his films, might no longer be as alive as passion or as dead as dreams, that they might become beings to whom his characters would attach themselves. That's how it was in real life: you got out of your chair and went to the sofa to join a half-asleep young woman whose sad gaze aroused tenderness.

Luca pulled Valérie to her feet and led her to the bedroom. "I'm sorry," he said, "but I'm exhausted. I haven't slept in two days."

He put her on the mattress, lay down beside her, and they made love. He knew he wasn't fooling her, and that she would have her own, quite definitive answers to any questions that might be asked about this nearly defunct relationship.

She shifted in the shadows as the rain beat against the windowpanes. She was stiff and tense. He took her by the waist and held her still. She shook herself free, rolled on top of him, and moved very slowly, murmuring, "This is it; we'll never be together again."

She held back her orgasm as long as she could.

Her face was tense; a tiny vein swelled in her cheek, just under the eye. She scratched his chest and told him again that this was the last time, that she wanted to brand him so he would never forget—and he never would, just as he had never forgotten any of the women whose names were gone with the years but whose mouths, gestures, and words he still recalled, not only for the love and the passion, but also by the traces left on his body, delicate, fleeting imprints whose scars he retained.

Valérie stretched out alongside him and asked, "Do you remember the first time?"

He said he did.

"And that time at the Brussels Métropole?"

"I remember," he said.

She'd been lying naked on the bed, drunk. He'd had three bottles of champagne sent up to the room and poured one over her. Her body was drenched with champagne, and she caressed herself through the bubbles and foam. Luca turned her over and emptied the second bottle on her back, and then she asked him to fuck her. That's exactly what she said, that one time and never again, like so many women embarrassed at letting themselves go to that extent: "Fuck me."

There was another time, during a boring dinner. They were sitting across from each other, and he took off his shoes and stroked her thighs with his bare foot while she chatted with the people sitting next to her. She tried to push him away, but he aroused her with his heel and toes, and she kept talking, sitting very straight, cheeks tinged red, perfectly convivial on the surface, wet and eager beneath, pressing her hips forward.

"And Madrid?" she asked. "Do you remember Madrid?"

But suddenly Luca crossed different borders, shaking off the mists of years and places. He recalled another story, an older one, with a woman Valérie didn't know. It happened during his first trip to St. Petersburg. Fleetingly it occurred to him that you might forget bodies and skins, but never great moments of pleasure. That was what he wished he could tell Valérie as she sat up and silently slipped on her nightgown. He looked at her, and sadness swept over him, a veil of bitterness interwoven with fatigue.

"You don't know how to keep a love alive very long," she said.

He didn't answer. He thought of the last time he'd seen Isabelle and of what she'd said to him. He thought of the night, in a Russian taxi, when he and Anna had marked each other forever. And as Valérie gently pulled the door closed behind her, he finally understood why he hadn't simply sat down at the girl's table in the dining car. He wanted to resurrect Anna one last time. To live the past in the present. And if they'd exchanged so much as one word, the mirages would have dissolved into another emotion. He didn't want that. What he wanted, for the last time, was for them to possess the infinite—a boundless empty space where they could rush toward each other with the same passion as before, when they met in the rain, at the café filled with students and chess players, at the ponds in Vésinet, in London, and in other places that had been theirs and that his memory had marked, joyful, tranquil surfaces upon which—and here was another dream—he could finally sleep.

When he awoke the city was transfixed in fog. A white cloud nibbled at the peak of Montparnasse tower. Below, cars crept along the avenue under the chestnut trees. He couldn't see or hear them, but he sensed their presence. He felt some joy at the thought that he would work all day and into the night, and even beyond, if he could.

But Luca was mistaken if he expected to spend the afternoon cocooned with words. On the kitchen table he found a note: "Boris Godunov phoned. Said he'd call back. I guess I won't be there, since it's winter. V."

He went into his office. On the wall above his desk was a glass-covered map of St. Petersburg. The Neva snaked through the city to the sea, flowing under bridges, meandering, wending its way among suburbs, streets, and houses, Anna's among them. Back in 1971, when Luca was released from the emergency room with a bandaged head and a broken spirit, he didn't know her address. He'd bought the map of Leningrad and pinned it to the wall of his room in The Garden. For weeks he stared at it, locating the places Anna had told him about, learning their names, whispering them to himself as he lay on his mattress at night. In the morning he would wait for the mail. When he realized no letter would come, he took his name off the box.

He applied to the film school. Besides a script, they wanted a portfolio of photographs. Luca submitted the portraits he'd done of Anna in the Saint-Germain forest.

He was accepted.

In late summer he put his meager belongings into two boxes and invited his few friends over. "Help yourselves," he told them.

The records, books, pillows, and dishes changed hands. Luca watched the pillage coolly, his back to the wall, arms folded, wearing a baggy sweater that hung down well below his hips. He felt no regret at scattering what little he possessed. He was simply cutting himself loose. The last traces of his childhood disappeared into alien hands, and he thought: May they make the best possible use of them.

When he left he wore his big black overcoat and the waterproof shoes he'd bought in London. He carried a battered leather suitcase held together with thongs. It was raining in the suburbs. The city smelled like mud. Luca left a sooty trail between the place he was now leaving and the new one he was going to, the film school, where he would regather what strength he had left. The soles of his shoes slapped loudly on the wet pavement. He was a gray shadow scurrying from a train to a métro station, from the métro to another train, and from that train to yet another suburb.

In 1975 Luca made the short film that allowed him to graduate from the film school with honors a few months later. He got a job interning on someone else's picture. He lived in a room on the top floor of a building in the eleventh arrondissement. He worked all day and often into the night, spending as many evenings as he could at the movies. He had no friends. He was so impassive about everything that anyone who came near him felt chilled. He had bolted and padlocked the door, losing himself in a welter of activities that kept his mind off himself. He filled the blank squares of his life by moving his pieces constantly, shifting from class to class, girl to girl, room to room, book to book.

On December 8 he turned twenty-three. He'd forgotten it was his birthday. When he came home from an old Billy Wilder film in black and white he found a letter in his mailbox. He stared at the envelope as he trudged up the six flights. Back in his room he sat on the mattress for a long time, legs crossed, back straight. Then, very slowly, he opened the envelope, unfolded the sheet of paper inside, and read the few words above the signature.

The next evening he landed in the city of Peter.

He was a little stunned by the massive blocks of concrete, the poverty and filth, and the shriveled grass and flickering, defective neon signs. It was a worn old world, he thought, a world utterly spent.

He waited a long time at passport control and finally showed his visa to an officer dressed in the legendary fur hat and long gray topcoat. He looked around disoriented, wondering whether she'd received his telegram. Then he saw her, just as he had that last time, through a glass partition. She had worked her way into a crowd that resembled a gallery of characters in a grisaille painting, an eager, curious throng in faded clothing watching the foreigners disembark. She was wearing the black sweater he'd bought her in London. Her eyes were wide, her forehead and hands pressed against the glass. There was a kind of incredulity in her look, a sort of dread. She stood there as her parents once had, waiting for him after the long separation.

He wanted to run to her, but there was yet another passport check. He stood to one side, clutching a metal guardrail, letting other passengers go by, staring at her, unable to take his eyes off the woman he had loved so much. He looked at her long dark hair, her matte complexion, and then he saw her lips move. She said something he couldn't make out, and her mouth widened into a broad smile.

He lost sight of her briefly while passing through the control point, but then he picked up his suitcase and started toward her, forgetting that there was a glass partition between them. In those days Russians were not allowed into the arrivals area.

He went closer.

They pressed themselves against the glass, eyes closed, hands searching, palms aligned one against the other. She didn't blink, but tears ran slowly down her cheeks, and he was touched by this joy that she could not contain, as though sloughing off all the old sadness now that he was here.

They went toward the exit, walking on either side of the glass. Luca knew he would shoot this scene exactly as it had taken place: she gliding along, palms blackened by the filthy glass, an expression of ineffable delight blossoming on her face, he, having left his suitcase behind, walking parallel to her, toward the door beyond which they would finally meet; then Luca bringing his hand softly to her cheek, caressing the skin, following her temple, descending along the cheekbone, brushing her lips as she kissed his fingertips, first without taking her eyes from his, and then, eyelids lowered, clutching his hand. He held her close, his arms around her, and rediscovered her embrace. He breathed in her perfume and thought to himself, She's my family, my only family. It was as if an amputated limb had been reattached, as if he could rest at last after so much torment.

They didn't speak, didn't kiss. They held each other, huddling close, smothering each other, fingers gripping the fabric of each other's clothing. He touched her hair, her neck. When they let go it was to stare into each other's eyes again—and to laugh, for someone was calling out to Luca, telling him to go back for his suitcase. He retrieved it, and they went out into the 4-degree-below-zero weather.

I've changed a lot," she said. "You probably don't even recognize me."

All at once she seemed burdened and joyless. "I wanted to see you," she added. "I wanted to see you so much!"

He wanted her to keep talking, wanted to be lulled forever by the husky voice he had missed so much.

They sat in a trolley bus on facing seats so they could look at each other. They passed the Bolsheokhtinski cemetery, the Naval Museum, and Moscow Station without ever taking their eyes off each other.

"You look so beautiful," she said.

He thought her face seemed lined. She was paler. She wore bright red lipstick that didn't suit her, a heavy woollen skirt frayed at the waist, thick tights, and a coarse navy-blue coat. The boots she'd bought in Paris were worn through, the soles cracked, split at the toe.

The elegant allure that always dazzled him when he saw her again after a few days' separation was gone. A sadness he'd never seen before flickered across her eyes like a veil of defeat and resignation. He wanted to take her in his arms and comfort her, make her forget. But when she let herself be drawn against him he felt a tiny contraction and had to hold her tight to make her let herself go again. Like before, like at the beginning.

She tried to ask questions as he kissed her forehead, her eyes, and finally her mouth.

Then they were together, really together, his hands on her cheeks, hers on the nape of his neck, and they rediscovered the inexpressible thoughts no phrase or gesture could convey better than their tongues, their lips, their teeth. Sighs and murmurs came to them as they touched, and their kisses shrank the space and abolished the time they'd spent apart.

The dilapidated trolley bus rolled down long, broad avenues lined by buildings reminiscent of the wretched apartment blocks of the Paris suburbs. Luca noticed several huge statues, dismal, dark, and ugly.

"I thought maybe you wouldn't love me anymore," Anna said, looking at him. "That maybe you'd forgotten me, and when you saw me again I'd be someone else, my old self, someone you never knew because in Paris I was already so different. People always turn into the city they live in. I was Paris, and you knew me as Paris, but now that's over and I'm Leningrad again. I'm Leningrad and I'm cold. Everyone's always cold in Leningrad."

They passed the governor's residence, the Mint, the Stroganov Palace. She took his hand and said, "This city is so beautiful, so imposing, but it has a human dimension because the buildings in the center are low and brightly colored. But it's a trap you can't get out of. Its poets always come back to sing its sadness and its sorrows. I'm like them. I can't live without this city, but it kills me when I'm in it."

She smiled faintly. The trolley bus came closer to the Neva, running along a wall behind which Luca glimpsed a monumental domed structure surmounted by a distant gold spire.

Anna pointed to the building. "The Peter and Paul Fortress," she said. "It's in all the books. It used to be a political prison. The history of the city begins right there, the day the architects laid the first stone. It's world famous, millions of tourists have seen it, and all Soviets know that one of its cannon fires a blank at noon every day, that during the siege mountain climbers covered the steeple of the cathedral to protect it from German bombs. Everyone knows all that—and also that it's where Peter the Great strangled his son with his own hands and that a hundred thousand people died building it. Peter and Paul is Leningrad."

They passed a bridge, the Field of Mars, the sea-green facade of the Winter Palace, the Admiralty, the Bronze Horseman. The trolley bus stopped, and they got off.

"I'm taking you to my place," Anna said, helping him pick up his suitcase.

They walked side by side, arm in arm, in silence, looking at Leningrad. They passed a theater, the Russian Museum, and a statue of Pushkin, his arm extended, scarf waving in the wind. An icy breeze ran along the bridges.

"I want you to love me again," Anna said. "I want you to try to love me again."

They came to the building where she lived. Three cars without windshield wipers were parked in front at an angle to the curb.

They went through a broad courtyard where a carpenter was hard at work and climbed a huge staircase of wood and concrete. The elevator was broken. The windows on the landings had no glass. Paint was peeling off the walls, and bulbs were gone from the sockets that hung from the ceilings.

At the top floor Anna stopped in front of a door

covered with dark leatherette. "I was born here," she said, turning to Luca. "It's a communal apartment. At least one other person will be here, maybe two."

They went into a narrow yellow hallway with black edging along the bottom. The floor was wood, the walls bare and recently scrubbed. Three pale rectangular patches bordered by dark outlines suggested that pictures had been removed.

They went into a long narrow room painted the same yellow as the hallway. In the center was an oak table with six perfectly aligned chairs. A lovely copper samovar stood on a buffet, there were a few prints on the wall, and a calendar hung above the buffet, near a door.

The door opened into a kitchen equipped with a gas cooker dating from the fifties. There was a cupboard and a counter with missing tiles. Near the window in a corner stood a man whose jacket blended into the walls. Luca was startled when he saw him, but the man didn't react. He held a cup in his hand and stared silent and unblinking at the newcomer.

"Come," Anna said.

She led him into a room he immediately recognized as hers and her parents'. Now emotion gripped him. Her dolls were there, and her toys, and photographs of Anna when she was a child. It was as though an unknown part of her had suddenly been revealed, as though all the things she'd told him about now came to life under his gaze. Touched, he looked at her little-girl secrets: a celluloid doll on a shelf, a few picture books, a pair of broken castanets, a hoop, a tiny white lace-up shoe she must have worn at the age of two or three. The bed, its frame painted pink and decorated with decals of flowers and little animals; a table with a blotter and blotting paper (streaked with the imprints of Cyrillic letters and lines from drawings that had been blotted there); colored pencils; an old magazine photo of Bob Dylan. Above the bed, to the left of the only window, was the Modigliani print of a woman with short brown hair cropped just above the arc of her eyebrow.

"Anna Akhmatova," Anna said, coming near him.

Luca put his arms around her. She let herself be held and whispered in his ear. "I used to share a room with the other couple's children," she said, "and my parents and their friends were in this room. When I left, my father put my things in here, and he and my mother had the room to themselves. She told me he had nightmares, and to fall asleep he would lie down on my bed where he could still smell my perfume. It depressed him that someday the last traces of his daughter would be gone, and when that day came, a long time later since he kept my scarfs under the pillow, he was deported to Siberia. Then he felt a new kind of pain."

She pulled away from him and turned the key in the lock.

"Who are the other tenants?" Luca asked.

"I don't know them. New ones came in not long ago, and I just got here."

"Where from?"

She was silent.

She showed him a child's drawing—Luca recognized the style immediately—and two photographs on the wall behind the door. One was of a woman, still young, leaning against the pillar of a bridge. Her eyes were lighter than her daughter's and she seemed taller, but she had the same smile and the same glint in her eyes. Luca saw a pale spot like a delicate imprint on her lip. "You have the same look in your eye," he said, "and that spot . . ."

"All the girls in my family have it. My grandmother, my mother, my aunt. My child will have it too, if I ever have one."

The man was sitting in an armchair with his daughter on his lap. He held a pad of paper and a pen. He was writing. The child was looking up at him, one finger in her mouth, the back of her left hand against her temple.

"He was writing a story for me. I was five. It

was a story about Arthur, a sly little man who was always fooling Komsomol bigshots."

Her father was blond and thin. He had a beard. He wore glasses. Anna didn't look like him.

"And that?" Luca asked, pointing to the drawing above the photographs.

"That," she said flatly, "is Gagarin."

They went to the kitchen. She made tea and served it in tiny earthenware cups. She sat across from him and watched him as he drank, watched him from below, her chin resting on her crossed forearms.

"Where are your parents?" Luca asked.

She shook her head. There were footsteps in the hallway, and a door slammed. Luca heard whispering in the other room. He put down his cup and held out his arms to Anna, who was now half lying on the table.

"Tell me whatever you feel like telling me," he murmured. "No more."

"My father's in a camp in eastern Siberia. My mother lives in a nearby kolkhoz. She goes to see him once a week."

She was silent for a moment, then added, "She's a cleaning lady now."

Luca waited a few seconds before asking the question she was waiting for, the one he'd had in his head since the first moment: "And you?"

She smiled faintly. "Talk to me," he insisted gently.

"I didn't forget you."

"That's not enough."

"I still draw."

"I'd like to see your drawings."

"They're not here."

"Where are they?"

She didn't answer. He got up and leaned against the window, looking down at the carpenter working in the courtyard below. An old man in woollen gloves. He stopped for a moment and waved at Luca.

"Where?"

"In Siberia," she said after a long silence.

She offered him more tea. He shook his head. He felt a knot in his chest. He knew now what tomorrow would bring.

A shadow moved in the other room. He went to the door and tried to close it, but the frame was warped.

"It doesn't matter," Anna whispered. "They don't understand what we're saying."

Luca let go of the knob. She smiled in resignation and added, "You have to get used to it."

He sat down across from her again and asked, "Where do you live?"

"With my mother."

She put her hand on his.

"I see my father every week. We try not to go together so he can have two visits instead of one, but my mother doesn't always get the authorization she needs. I meet him in the courtyard, with a fence between us. We don't say anything. We can never bring ourselves to talk. We just stare at each other and hold hands through the fence. I wanted to tell him about you, but I couldn't, because I was ashamed that we had what we had in a city so different, the city they sent me to, all our dreams and happiness. So I didn't tell him. But I think about you. I think about you all the time."

$\mathcal{H}$e gave her the presents he'd brought from Paris: a short coat, a tight black dress, stockings, a pair of loafers.

She left him to get dressed in the bedroom. When she came back she was radiant. Like in London and Paris. It took so little for everything to be like before. So little: London or Paris.

They went out. She showed him the Smolny monastery, with its white cupola and golden spire, and the soft, pastel facades she had described for him so perfectly.

"I thought there were two cities inside me," she said, "and that they had somehow merged. Paris and Leningrad. But when I was with you, Leningrad gnawed at me—that's the word, that's exactly the word—and here I feel orphaned from Paris."

"Come back with me," Luca said without thinking.

She put her finger to his lips to silence him.

"When I came back," she said, "I realized I was wrong, and that if I wanted to live, even just a little, I had to forget one of those two worlds—forget it and mourn it. I had no choice. It had to be Paris. Because it was easier."

They were passing the Neva. The river was frozen. Luca sensed that Anna was holding something back.

"It's not the cities," he replied. "It's your father, your mother, and me. The past and the future."

But he knew that beyond this agony lay a third,

missing term, one that could reconcile the contradictions. Some major element was missing. But she would not express it.

They crossed a drawbridge which, she explained, was raised at night, isolating Leningrad's center from its outskirts. They crossed back to the other side of the river and passed stores with empty shelves and others with long lines.

"I know you can't fully understand it," Anna went on, "but I feel tied to my parents, to this city, and to the misery of the people who live here."

They walked along the Nevsky Prospekt, with its crowded sidewalks and trolley-bus cables suspended overhead like a net. Luca thought about all the questions he could ask, all the things that inevitably occur to you in situations like these, breaking the surface like bubbles on dark water. They were doomed. That's what she was saying.

They passed Palace Square. Luca looked at the Alexander Column and the surrounding buildings. Then they returned to the courtyard. The carpenter had packed up for the day. They climbed the broad staircase and went back into the overheated apartment, to the room she'd had as a little girl. For the first time she was the one who took the initiative, pushing him onto the bed, undressing him, putting him inside her with a volition he'd never seen her show before. She clapped her hand over his mouth to keep him from moaning, and she gave and took in utter silence broken only by noises from the other side of the wall. In the end they ignored them. They were together, and it didn't matter if others could hear or see them. And so they remained all day and all night, and the next day and evening too, until two hours before it was time for him to go.

They took a taxi to the station. She wore the clothes he'd brought her from Paris. Earlier, as she hitched the stockings to the garter belt, she'd said, "I'm like a woman now."

"Why did you ask me to come?" he asked as they sat in the taxi.

"To see you."

"That's not the only reason."

"No," she said, "it's not."

Suddenly there was a touch of something like

madness in her voice. Something he'd never heard before.

She took his hand and brought it to her thigh, shaped by the sheath of the stocking. He scratched lightly with his fingernails, sliding his hand down to rest on her kneecap.

"Maybe one day you'll understand," she said.

His fingertips brushed the back of her knee. She began to draw his hand higher, but all at once she wanted something else. "I want something else," she said, and he answered, "Do what you want."

She leaned back against the seat and opened her legs slightly. The driver could see nothing.

She began to move, slowly at first. Luca moved his hand. She took it and put it exactly where she wanted. She raised herself up, breathing faster, her lips parted. Her fingers were tight on his hand. She turned her head to the window as though trying to put the taxi, her lover, and all of reality out of her mind, finally abandoning herself to pure desire. An obscene, violent despair swept over him. He wanted to make her come, to feel her come under his hand, without moving any more than he had to.

He lifted the skirt, stroked the bare flesh above the top of her stocking, moving just a little higher, and then she slipped off her pants, arched her back, and opened her legs wide, planting her feet on the back of the front seat, exposing herself to the moonlight and the street lamps.

She turned her head toward Luca, opened her eyes, and said, "Do it again, do it with your fingers." She moaned as he put them inside her, first one, then two. She pressed herself forward, setting the rhythm she wanted, keeping her hand on Luca's, clawing his skin when he pretended to take his hand away to make her wait again.

He knew what she wanted. She was acting as if she had to engrave him inside herself, to keep forever something of this man who would soon be leaving her, as though trying to absorb the very last trace of what would one day become a great love, an immense love—a love gone dead.

She murmured insults at him, vulgarities that made him want to slap her.

"Make the taxi stop," she said. "I want you to fuck me."

They were in the frozen grounds of the English Park. He suddenly wondered whether she'd brought him there deliberately.

The taxi stopped in a deserted alleyway. She opened the door, closed it behind her, walked off into the shadows, leaned against a tree trunk, and waited for him. He lifted her skirt and penetrated her standing up, her silk-sheathed legs wrapped around his hips, with a brutality that provoked hers, their eyes wide to watch each other come and to remember it.

Two hours later, just before he boarded the train that would take him back to Paris, she said, "Someday you might get a letter from me."

"When?" he asked.

"In ten years."

three

It was dark out when the phone rang in his office. Luca picked up the receiver and recognized the voice immediately.

"I have the address you wanted."

He felt a knot in his stomach. He sat down.

"She didn't get off in Poznań or Brussels. She's in Paris."

His fingers trembled slightly as he took a pen and pad. Perhaps out of superstition, he tried to postpone the moment. "Where are you calling from?" he asked.

But the other party parried the thrust. "It's not a house or hotel. If you had her in mind for the role of the girl, it looks like you hit the nail on the head."

"What do you mean?"

"The address is a theater."

"Give it to me."

He wrote it down. He wanted to thank him with a few kind words, but the actor-conductor hung up.

Luca called a cab.

He remembered.

He'd gone back to Leningrad in 1977. Anna's family had disappeared. The top-floor apartment had been requisitioned. The carpenter was still hard at work in the courtyard, but he had no idea where the girl had gone. Neither did anyone else.

Over the next few years he tried again several times, with no luck. On his last trip the carpenter was gone. Luca paid someone to open up the apartment and let him in, but he found nothing. The walls were a

different color. Some of the partitions had been torn
down. Other people had been living there for a long
time. That was in 1985. Ten years after his visit. The
year he got Anna's letter.

It came to him by an extraordinary route, via a
messenger he hadn't seen since the day long ago when
she and Anna ran into each other in front of The
Garden.

He was in New York for the opening of his latest
film, and one morning he got a call in his hotel room
from that forgotten friend: Isabelle. She was an inter-
preter now. She happened to be passing through New
York and read in the papers that he was in town. She
asked to see him. She had something to tell him.

He invited her to dinner.

That evening he waited for her in the hotel
lobby.

He remembered a charming, self-assertive
woman with very dark eyes and thin lips, and when
she entered the lobby, he quickly recognized those few
highlights that had not faded from his memory. She
looked the same, but different. She had a very wise,
almost serene beauty now. White silk dress, polished
high heels, manicured nails. But her dark gaze pierced
him as though erasing time and plunging to his eigh-
teen-year-old heart, to the bed where he'd taken her,
in the widow's house.

They looked at each other from a distance, in silence. He took a step, she took one, and they both said, "You haven't changed a bit," the way people always do in such situations.

They dined on pink champagne.

She told him about her life and he told her about his.

"I knew we'd see each other again someday," she said.

And he said, "You're as beautiful as ever."

She was barely thirty and had the smile, style, and voice of a woman who'd been around. But traces of the little girl he once knew streaked through his memory and piqued his senses. She was charming, tough, and expert in the use of that magnificent dark gaze. She had very thin lips that seemed dry.

In his room the next morning she said, "I was on a job in Moscow ten days ago, and a woman came to the embassy."

Luca took her by the shoulder. A vague uneasiness slid between them.

"What woman?" he breathed.

"Her," Isabelle replied.

He didn't react. He felt drained. His limbs went numb before the breakfast tray.

"Her," Isabelle repeated. "Anna."

She sat down in front of him.

"It was a coincidence. An incredible coincidence. She asked me to mail a letter from Paris, and the letter was for you. It was like a message in a bottle in the ocean. I told her I knew you a long time ago, when I was just a kid. That was when she recognized me. But I didn't remember her. It seems we met at the door of your room at The Garden."

Luca nodded. He didn't care about that. He wanted to know the rest.

"Did you talk?"

"Yes."

"Why was she writing to me?"

"I can't tell you."

She put her hand on his arm and added, very gently, as if to soften a cruel blow, "You'll read it. It's her secret. She wanted to tell you herself."

"How long did you talk?"

"All night."

"How is she?" Luca asked, feeling suddenly confused. "Where is she living? Is she alone?"

Isabelle shook her head.

"I can't tell you anything. She didn't want me to. She made me promise."

She got up and went to the door. Her coat was hanging from a hook.

"She's alive. That's what counts."

She took the coat off the hook. Luca stood up and went to her.

"Tell me what she looked like. I mean, when you first saw her."

"She was in the middle of a crowd at the embassy gate. I noticed her because she was holding a letter, waving it frantically. She seemed incredibly distressed, so I went over to her. She asked me in Russian whether I knew you. I looked at the envelope. Your name was on it, but there was no address. I told her I'd take care of it. Then she lowered her eyes and just stood there, her arms hanging at her sides. She had on a very old black coat, wretched galoshes, and gloves with the fingertips cut off. She was crying."

Isabelle slipped an arm into the sleeve of her coat. Luca couldn't bring himself to help her.

"She was crying with relief, like an exhausted, ravaged woman finally getting to her destination after terrible suffering. I took her to a hotel where it was warm."

Isabelle buttoned her coat. Luca hadn't moved.

"Where's the letter?" he asked.

"I sent it to your production company."

"When?"

"Just before I came here. Three days ago."

She left him her phone number in New York. "I'll call you," he said.

But he didn't. The next day he caught the first plane to Paris.

In the taxi to the theater he thought of Anna's letter. Five hundred words. In her tiny, round handwriting, in violet ink, she explained why she had asked him to come to Leningrad ten years before. It was time to confess, she said.

Ten years: that was the deadline she'd set.

She had now kept her word, thereby nailing shut the coffin of their story forever and ever.

Luca paid the taxi and got out. It wasn't a theater but a concert hall. It took him a long time to talk his way in, and the moment he passed through the door he recognized the piece being played. Her interpretation was not unlike Wanda Landowska's.

Something seemed to shift inside him. Two images assailed him, one gradually superimposing itself over the other, like a tracing. He stopped. He leaned against the wall, in the shadow of the final act. He wanted to move forward but found he couldn't, wanted to call out a name but didn't know it. Who would he tell, and what for?

He waited, following the play of shadows from the stalls to the orchestra, staring at row upon row of velvet seats, not daring to go any farther. Then suddenly he thought he might lose her again. Once in the train, once in this concert hall. So he moved down the side aisle, toward the front rows.

The pianist was sitting in profile, playing Beethoven's *Funeral March*.

Luca went closer. Not far from the piano he bent down on one knee. The girl looked coolly elegant in her performance clothes: an austere, dark jacket, white dress, gray stockings, patent leather shoes. She was wearing the black shawl that had covered her shoulders in the dining car. She played with impressive self-control, leaning close to the keyboard, head swaying slightly left and right, torso immobile, fingers flying over the keys, elbows tight against her sides. Her eyes were half closed. Just before she began the third movement, *Marcia funebre sulla morte d'un eroe*, she fleetingly raised her hand to the nape of her neck, tilted her head back, and brought her forearm to her cheek.

Luca knew every note, every inflection, of that sonata. He had looked for a recording of it everywhere. Yet now he barely heard it. Different music was playing inside him. An aria for three voices, one of which was missing. A half note, a quarter note, a sigh. Off to the side of the front row, one knee to the floor, the other trembling slightly under his arm, yet somehow very calm, Luca looked at his daughter.

about the author

Dan Franck is the author of numerous screenplays and novels. *Separation,* his previous novel, was published in the United States in 1994. The film was directed by Christian Vincent and starred Isabelle Huppert and Daniel Auteuil, with a screenplay by the author. Mr. Franck lives in Paris.

about the translator

Jon Rothschild's translation of Dan Franck's *Separation* received wide acclaim. His other translations include Alain Peyrefitte's *The Immobile Empire* and a forthcoming biography of Georges Simenon. He is a longtime resident of New York City.